# HENRY HOLLINS AND
# THE DINOSAUR

D1585920

# HENRY HOLLINS AND THE DINOSAUR

WILLIS HALL

Illustrated by John Griffiths

**A TARGET BOOK**
*published by*
the Paperback Division of
W. H. Allen & Co. Ltd

A Target Book
Published in 1978
by the Paperback Division of W. H. Allen & Co. Ltd
A Howard & Wyndham Company
44 Hill Street, London W1X 8LB

Reprinted, 1978

First published in Great Britain by
The Bodley Head Ltd, 1977, under the title,
THE SUMMER OF THE DINOSAUR

Copyright © by Willis Hall, 1977
Illustrations copyright © by The Bodley Head Ltd, 1977

Printed in Great Britain by
Richard Clay (The Chaucer Press), Ltd,
Bungay, Suffolk

ISBN 0 426 20043 8

This book is sold subject to the condition that it
shall not, by way of trade or otherwise, be lent,
re-sold, hired out or otherwise circulated without
the publisher's prior consent in any form of
binding or cover other than that in which it is
published and without a similar condition
including this condition being imposed on the
subsequent purchaser.

# HENRY HOLLINS AND
# THE DINOSAUR

# I

The angry, flapping, grey-green dragon dipped its ugly head and charged off across the sky, as though setting out in pursuit of the thin skein of snow-white clouds that hung low on the horizon. The boy on the beach shaded his eyes from the sun with his free hand, and gazed up above his head at the roving monster. In his mind's eye it became a sharp-toothed pterodactyl wheeling over the restless sea in search of food, ever-ready to turn and dip and dive and spear an unsuspecting fish that cruised beneath the surface of the water.

"Henry!" The voice of the boy's mother broke in on his thoughts. "You won't go *too* near the water's edge, will you, dear?"

"No, Mum!" he yelled back, taking his attention away from his gaily painted kite for a moment, and shouting across the beach to where his parents were sitting.

"And *try* not to wander too close to the cliffs, darling," his mother continued. "They're *very* dangerous."

"I won't."

"And you will promise me that you won't play in the rock-pools, won't you, Henry? You'll only get

7

your feet wet, and you *know* how bad you are at shaking off a cold!"

"All right!"

"And you won't stray too far away, Henry, will you? The tide is on the turn and we wouldn't want to see you marooned on the rocks!"

"I won't!"

Mrs Emily Hollins smiled comfortably, took her eyes off her only child, picked up yet another envelope from the box at her feet and quickly scribbled a name and address across the front.

Albert Hollins, Emily's husband, glanced up from his newspaper crossword and frowned at his wife. "What *are* those envelopes?" he asked. "And what are you writing on them?"

"I'm addressing them, dear," said Emily Hollins, "for charity."

"Yes, I thought you might be," said Albert, with a sigh. Emily Hollins spent a great deal of her time doing things for charity: when she wasn't addressing envelopes she was pinning paper flags on people's coats, and when she wasn't pinning paper flags on people, she was quite often collecting old clothes for poor people all over the world. "Which charity are you addressing envelopes for?" asked Albert.

"I'm not quite sure," said Emily, "but I do know that it's in aid of a very good cause."

"Yes," said Albert, and he sighed again, "I'm sure it must be." Only a couple of days before Albert had discovered, to his horror, that Emily had taken his cricket bat on behalf of some people who were in need of food and clothing in some distant corner of the world. Albert was all in favour of giving people food and clothing, but he didn't see the point in sending them his cricket bat. "They can't eat it," he muttered to himself, "or wear it on their heads." Albert Hollins let out his third sigh of the afternoon, and tried to concentrate on his crossword puzzle, but his wife's voice broke in again on his thoughts.

"I've told Henry to keep away from the sea, *and* not to climb the cliffs, *and* to keep out of the rock-pools *and* not to go wandering off anywhere by himself," she said.

"Humph," replied Mr Hollins, his pencil hovering over his newspaper. "All I want now," he went on, "is a word of three letters beginning with 'n' which means to scold, grumble, or continually find fault."

"Nag, dear," said Emily Hollins brightly.

"Jolly good," said Mr Hollins, and he filled in the word in his puzzle and sat back in his folding chair. "What was that you said about Henry?" he asked.

Mrs Hollins sighed and said again, "I've told him to keep out of the sea, away from the cliffs, not to get his feet wet, and to keep in sight."

"Well done, Emily," said Mr Hollins. "I should think you've covered every possible contingency there for accident. Where is he, by the way?"

"Who?"

"Our Henry. Where has he got to and what is he doing?"

Mrs Hollins peered around the small cove they were sitting in and her mouth dropped open in surprise. There was no sign of Henry anywhere. "That boy!" she said, shaking her head in disbelief. "He's doing just what I told him not to do—he's wandering off, by himself."

"I shouldn't worry," said Albert Hollins, and he pointed up into the blue sky overhead where Henry's kite, with the colourful dragon design, wheeled and fluttered and dipped and curled, tugged by the breeze. "As long as we can see that, we'll know exactly where he is."

"All the same," said Emily, "I do wish he would do as he's told—it would make life easier." She glanced down at the boxful of envelopes. "I've got more than enough on my plate."

"Speaking of plates," said Mr Hollins, "what kind of sandwiches have we got left?"

Emily opened a number of plastic boxes and scrabbled about in their contents like an inquisitive hamster. "There's some eggy ones," she said, "and some cheesy ones, and just one salmon-and-cucumber one."

"Salmon and cucumber, that's for me!" said Albert, smacking his lips in anticipation. Emily Hollins handed the last of the salmon-and-cucumber sandwiches to her husband, who took a large bite and then spat it out. "It's got sand in it," he grumbled.

"Oh, that reminds me!" said Emily. "I've got a flag-day next Saturday for those people in the Sahara Desert."

But Albert Hollins was too hungry himself at that moment to consider the plight of poor people in other parts of the world. "What about the eggy sandwiches and the cheesy ones?" he asked. "Have they got sand in them as well?"

Emily Hollins scrabbled about again in her plastic boxes. "I'm afraid so," she said at last, "and there's sand on top of the custard tart."

Albert Hollins blew out his breath peevishly. He had been looking forward particularly to a piece of custard tart. "I suppose it's time we were thinking of making a move for home," he said. "We've got to get all our things into the car. If we leave it until too late before we set off, we're sure to get stuck in all kinds of traffic. There are thousands of day-trippers on the popular beaches just along the coast." He rose to his feet, folded up his chair, and dusted the sand from his trousers.

"Whatever you say, Albert," said Mrs Hollins. "I'll just call Henry and he can help us pack everything and—" she broke off, and then: "Oh, dear!" she said.

"What is it now?" growled Mr Hollins.

In answer, Emily Hollins pointed up into the sky.

11

"It's Henry's kite," said Mrs Hollins. "It isn't there any longer."

Mr Hollins blew out his breath again and stamped his feet. "That boy", he said, "is never around when he's wanted. Where's he got to now?"

"I don't know, dear," said Mrs Hollins. "He was on the other end of the kite, when it was up in the sky. But now that the kite has disappeared, I'm afraid I don't know where Henry is."

"You should have told him not to wander off," grumbled Mr Hollins.

"I did do," said Mrs Hollins, stoutly. "Don't you remember? I told him not to stray away too far, not to go near the sea, and not to climb up cliffs."

"Then whatever you told him *not* to do, he's sure to go off and do it," observed Mr Hollins, gloomily. "He'll most likely drift away for a couple of hours, soak himself to the skin in sea-water, and tear his trousers climbing cliffs." Mr Hollins puffed out both his cheeks and slowly let the air out of his lips, resentfully. Although his angry words were directed at his son, they were spoken with all the bitter frustration of a man who has discovered sand in his salmon-and-cucumber sandwich and also found it on top of his custard tart.

Words failed Albert Hollins and he stood staring sadly out to sea for almost a minute. Mrs Hollins bit her lip and said nothing; she had been married to Mr

Hollins long enough to recognize his moods, and she knew when it was better to keep silent.

"Come on then, let's get this lot cleared away," muttered Mr Hollins at last, indicating the debris of their day by the sea, which included: two folding chairs with a matching folding table, travelling rugs, vacuum flasks (one for tea and one for tomato soup), newspapers, magazines, the large box of envelopes, dirty plates, cups and cutlery, and a selection of sand-infested sandwiches.

Mrs Hollins bent down and began to pick things up.

Mr and Mrs Hollins and their son, Henry, lived in a house called Woodview, which was the end one in a row of similar neat houses on the outskirts of a small town called Staplewood.

Staplewood had a High Street which contained: a Woolworth's, a Marks and Spencer's, two supermarkets, one cinema, a Bingo Hall, eighty-four various kinds of shops, a Gas Board office, an Electricity Showroom, nine public houses and an oak-beamed hotel called the Pig and Bucket. The owners of the Pig and Bucket Hotel preferred it to be known as an old coaching inn. It was said that Charles Dickens had spent a part of his life, and written a part of a book, at the Pig and Bucket. No one knew exactly how long Mr Dickens had spent at the Pig and Bucket—some said four weeks, others said six months—or which one of his many famous novels he had worked on during his stay in Staplewood; some said *Little Dorrit,* others said *Dombey and Son.*

As a matter of fact, there were some doubting citizens of Staplewood who would tell you that Mr Dickens' stay at the Pig and Bucket had been no more than an overnight one. And that his only contribution to English literature during his brief visit had been an uncomplimentary jotting in the Pig and Bucket visitors' book: "Very hard peas and similar bed." Nevertheless, nobody could deny that Charles Dickens had spent *some* time in Staplewood, no matter how short. And so the town had gained some slight fame as a tourist attraction. During the summer months, many people, some of them Americans, came to Staplewood and visited the Pig and Bucket. They paused there to peer in at the bedroom where Mr Dickens had laid his head. During July and August, Staplewood High Street was thronged with tourists who not only peeked in at the Dickens bedroom, but also visited the cinema and the Bingo Hall. Some of them even gazed solemnly at the electric blankets and coffee percolators in the window of the Electricity Showroom—even though there was nothing in the town's records to show that Charles Dickens had had anything to do with the cinema or the Bingo Hall or even the Electricity Showroom.

Yet for all the entertainments and delights of Staplewood High Street, there was one holiday attraction that was not on offer to the discerning holiday-maker: Staplewood did not possess a beach. Not that this was in any way surprising, for Staplewood, as any map would show, was situated over thirty-five miles from the sea. And so, while the pleasant country town proved a popular stopping-off place for foreign tourists, country-lovers in general, and Charles Dickensites in particular, the residents of the town themselves were inclined to look elsewhere when they went in search of relaxation.

The Hollins family was not the only one in Staplewood that preferred the pleasures of the beach to those of the countryside. Which was why, on any sunny, summer Sunday morning, you would see a queue of slowly moving cars journeying out of Staplewood and on to the motorway that led towards the sea. And also why, on any sunny, summer Sunday evening, you might also see that same queue, in reverse order, moving back, snail-like, to Staplewood. Which also goes to explain why Albert Hollins, who did not like traffic jams, was always anxious to be sitting behind the wheel of his family car, heading back along the motorway, before the tip of the setting sun had touched the sea.

Emily Hollins examined the custard tart and pursed her lips. "I think it's all right now, Albert," she said. "I've scraped all the sand from off the top,

15

and I don't think that any of it has managed to get *inside* the custard."

Albert Hollins took the custard tart from out of Emily's hands and gazed at it, morosely. There were little criss-cross knife-marks all over the custard where Emily had scraped off the sand. "No, thanks," muttered Albert, "I can't really say that I fancy it any longer."

"I don't see why not," said Emily. "There are *some* people, in *some* parts of the world, who would be extremely grateful for that custard tart."

"They're welcome to it then," said Albert, and he drew back his arm and threw the custard tart far and high and out towards the sea. The custard tart soared up and up and then, before it could begin its downward path, a screaming seagull wheeled and dived from out of the evening sky, snatched up the custard tart in its beak and flew off.

"Goodness!" exclaimed Emily. "That just reminds me! I have to take a collecting box round next Tuesday night for the O.F.F.F."

"What's the O.F.F.F.?" asked Albert.

"Our Feathered and Furry Friends, of course," said Emily.

Albert Hollins shook his head, slowly, frowned out at the sea, and changed the subject. "Where has that boy got to?" he said. "Just look at the time! That motorway will be head-to-tail with traffic all the way from here to Staplewood."

16

"Why don't you go and look for him?" said Emily.

"I'm going to," said Albert. "And when I find him, he'll find himself in very hot water."

But Henry Hollins was in hot water at the same moment that his father had uttered those words.

Henry Hollins was stuck up a cliff. And not only was the lad marooned and alone up a steep cliff-face—he was alone and marooned with sopping-wet socks and feet, and also with a large rip in his trousers' seat.

What had happened was this: a few minutes earlier, Henry's kite had taken a sudden tumble out of the sky and had nose dived half-way down the cliff-face. Henry, in headlong flight across the beach in pursuit of the kite, had run straight through a rock-pool; had tripped over a giant-sized pebble; had torn his trousers on a piece of broken shell; had succeeded in scrambling half-way up the side of the cliff and had, at last, come to a full stop on a narrow ledge where he now stood, rested, and assessed his situation.

The kite was up above his head, way out of reach and un-get-at-able. The shingle beach was far below and, although he had managed to scramble his way up, in his excitement, he was not at all sure that he would be able to make his way down again.

"First things first, though," said Henry Hollins to himself, as he summoned up his courage and decided to make his final assault on the cliff-face to retrieve the kite.

17

He stretched up his arm and found a firm hand-hold somewhere up above his head. Next, he raised a cautious foot on to an outjutting piece of rock and then pressed down on it, testing the foot-hold before trusting it with all his weight. It was lucky for Henry that he did make this preliminary test, for as his foot pressed down on the rock he felt it give way beneath him and he heard, rather than saw, a chunk of rock crumble off and hurtle down, breaking into fragments as it struck the cliff-face, and finally rattle in a thousand tiny pieces on the shingle at the foot of the cliff.

Henry gulped twice and then slowly, ever so slowly, eased his foot back on to the overhanging ledge. He then lowered his hand, gave a sigh of relief, and made up his mind to wait a couple of minutes before starting another attempt on the cliff. He squatted down on the safety of the ledge. Then he paused, blinked, and blinked again. He found himself gazing at a curious object that seemed to be stuck, half in and half out of the rock where the chunk had broken off under the weight of his foot.

The boy peered closely at the object which, at first sight, appeared to be perfectly round, was about twenty centimetres in diameter, and was a browny-grey colour. He put out his hand and ran his fingers over the ball-like object. He found it smooth to his touch.

At first, he wondered if it was a cannon-ball that

18

had been fired from a marauding galleon centuries before, and had been lodged in the rock-face ever since. But he had come across cannon-balls before: both in museums and stacked as relics on castle battlements. He knew that cannon-balls were only about fifteen centimetres across. Besides, cannon-balls were made of iron, and somehow the object didn't *feel* like metal.

Next, he wondered if it might be a large piece of rock or some strange kind of mineral. But the object didn't seem to have that kind of feel about it either—also, he had never seen a rock that was so perfectly round before.

Henry Hollins could not decide what the object was. He was almost ready to give up, and set off after his kite again, when he realized something else. As he allowed his hands to run over the smooth surface of whatever it was, he discovered that the object *wasn't* stuck in the rock at all. It was quite loose. If he levered it gently with his hands, he realized, it would come free.

Slowly and ever so carefully, Henry Hollins eased the object out of the rock-face, keeping his hands underneath it as he did so, to take the weight. And the thing slipped out of its niche in the cliff even more easily than the boy had thought that it would. Within seconds, he was cradling the thing in his arms, examining it more closely. He found out that it wasn't as heavy as he had imagined it would be, and that it wasn't completely round either. One end of it was round, the part that had been sticking out of the cliff, but the end that had been hidden in the rock came almost to a point. And now that he held the complete object he realized that instead of being like a ball, as he had thought it was, it was really ... well ... egg-shaped.

Henry Hollins' heart began to beat a little faster than was normal. He was holding in his arms a browny-grey egg-like thing that was about thirty-five centimetres long and twenty centimetres across.

He *knew* what it was. Which was strange, for he had never seen one before in his life. Indeed, to the best of his knowledge there was not another one like it in the world.

He felt a tingling feeling of excitement at the back of his throat and the hairs began to prickle along his neck. He was aware of the quickening of his own breath.

Henry Hollins clutched the object closer to his chest. He was trying to clasp it tightly so as not to drop it and, at the same time, hold it more gently for fear that it might shatter in his grasp.

The boy blinked his eyes three times, quickly, to make sure that he was awake and that what was happening was real. He told himself that his name was Henry Hollins, that he lived at Woodview, Nicholas Nickleby Close, Staplewood, and that at that precise moment in time he was standing half-way up a cliff, on a ledge, and clutching in his arms something that was completely priceless and unique. For it was, without a shadow of a doubt, a perfect specimen of a fossilized dinosaur's egg.

# 2

Henry Hollins knew quite a lot about dinosaurs, for prehistoric life was his favourite subject, and he borrowed all the books about it from his local library. He liked to read about the mighty *Diplodocus,* the lumbering *Brontosaurus,* the ferocious *Antrodemus,* and *Tyrannosaurus Rex,* the largest and most terrible of all dinosaurs. His own particular favourite dinosaur was the spiky *Stegosaurus.* He had built a model of a *Stegosaurus* and it was the centrepiece of the Henry Hollins' Prehistoric Museum, which was situated in his father's tool shed at the bottom of the garden. He knew quite a lot about fossils too. He had spent a holiday the previous year in a Dorset village by the sea, and had managed to collect some fine ammonite specimens. These were also on display in his private museum. And there were other exhibits that he had bought with pocket money from a collectors' shop: a trilobite fossil and a couple of belemnites which he believed to be over 250,000,000 years old.

But all of these previously prized possessions seemed like common-or-garden objects compared with the one that he now held tightly to his chest. Henry Hollins closed his eyes, hugged the giant fossil egg, and tried to wish himself back into a distant age

when gigantic, clumsy prehistoric monsters ruled the earth.

"*Come* along! Wake up! Dreamy Daniel! *You!*"

A complaining voice brought Henry back to the present day, and he opened his eyes and looked down at the foot of the cliff. An angry figure glared up at him, hands on hips, grimly furious.

"Hello Dad," said Henry Hollins.

"Is that *all* you've got to say?" said Albert. "What do you think you're up to, eh? Sitting half-way up a cliff with your eyes closed. Have you got the slightest *idea* what the time is?"

Henry shook his head. "I came up here to get my kite," he said.

"I don't know," said Albert. "I really just don't know at all. You'd better come down then—jump to it."

"I can't," said Henry. "I'm stuck."

"Stuck? Stuck? Stuck?" Mr Hollins repeated the word three times, as if he had never heard the collection of letters before. "Stuck how? Stuck where?"

"Stuck up here, Dad," said Henry. "I can't get down."

"You got yourself up there, didn't you?"

"Yes, Dad."

"Then you can get yourself down again," said Mr Hollins. "There's going to be a queue of cars fifty

25

miles long, from here to Staplewood, by the time we hit that motorway. What's that you're holding?"

"What?"

"*That!* In your hands, Henry. What is it?"

"Oh, this!" said Henry, looking down at the dinosaur's egg. His father's sudden appearance had made the boy forget his discovery. "It's a fossil, Dad. Look." And Henry held up the egg for his father to see.

"Fossil? Fossil? They're *old*, aren't they?"

"Very old, Dad," Henry called down the cliff-face. "Millions and millions of years old, as a matter of fact."

"Yes, I thought they were," said Albert. "You don't want to fill your head up with the past, Henry. Look ahead—not back. Think of where you're going to be tomorrow."

"Still up on this ledge, Dad, if you don't rescue me."

Albert Hollins shook his head with pretended long-suffering at the waywardness of his only son. "There's a rope in the boot of the car," he said. "I'll go and get it."

"Thanks, Dad."

"And I'll come back to the top of the cliff with it and pull you up—that'll be easier for you than climbing down."

"Thanks, Dad."

"Shan't be long; don't go away." Albert Hollins

chuckled at his own joke. Then, as he took a last look up at his son, his face clouded over. The moods of Mr Hollins were as changeable as the summer weather. "Are you all wet?" he asked.

"Only my shoes and socks, Dad," said Henry. "I ran through a rock-pool."

"And is that a tear in your trousers?"

"Just a little one—I caught them on a piece of broken shell."

"I don't know how you manage to do it, Henry, I really don't," said Albert. "Look at me. I've been here on the beach, all day, *just* as long as you, but have *I* managed to get myself into a mess?"

Henry gazed down at the neat and tidy figure of his father on the beach and said nothing. There were knife-edge creases in Albert Hollins' white linen trousers. Albert Hollins' suede shoes were unscuffed and looked, in fact, as if they had just been taken out of their box. The check shirt that Albert Hollins was wearing was crisp and clean and just as much a credit to Emily's ironing as it had been the moment that he had first slipped it on. There was not so much as a single hair out of place on Albert Hollins' slightly balding head.

"I said, have I managed to get myself into a mess?" Albert repeated his question.

"No, Dad."

"I honestly don't know how you manage to do it,"

said Albert and, shaking his head sadly, he set off back across the beach the way he had come.

"Dad!" yelled Henry Hollins after his father.

"What?"

"What are we going to do about this?" Henry was holding up the dinosaur's egg.

"Throw it away."

"Throw it away?" Henry Hollins was staggered at his father's suggestion. "But it's a dinosaur's egg, Dad! It's a valuable fossil! It's probably over two hundred million years old!"

"I don't care if it's a new-laid duck egg!" yelled back Albert Hollins. "You're not taking that great thing home in my car, I only vacuumed it out this morning. Besides, you've filled up my garden shed with more than enough useless rubbish as it is!"

"But, Dad . . ."

It was no use. Albert Hollins had turned his back on Henry. The boy watched his father's stern, retreating figure, and frowned.

No matter what his father had said, he was not going to give up the dinosaur fossil if he could possibly help it. He glanced down the cliff-face and bit his lip. He wondered if he *could* get down again? By himself? Before his father got back? He *had* managed to get up by himself, it was true. But even if he did make the return trip unaided, how was he going to get the fossil down as well? He would need both his hands for the climb down. He chewed again at his lower lip and thought hard and fast. A possible solution occurred to him. Then, without wasting any time, he put his idea into action.

He took off his jacket and knotted the sleeves together. Next he slipped his head through the loop he had made, forming a sort of clumsy rucksack that rested high on his back. Then he took the fossil in both hands, lifted it over his head and tucked it in, carefully, among the folds of his jacket. He took his hands away and, gingerly, holding his breath, wriggled his shoulder-blades. The fossil stayed put, lodged insecurely between his jacket and his back. He could feel the tip nuzzling against the back of his head. And, although it didn't feel very secure, he knew that it was the best he could manage under the circumstances. He would have to move fast if he was going to get down the cliff before his father came back.

Taking a firm hand-hold on a crevice in the cliff, keeping his neck perfectly still, he lowered first one foot and then the other. His free hand felt across the rock-face, seeking and finding another niche. He lowered his body again, one foot first and then the other, slowly . . .

As things turned out, going down the cliff was not half as dangerous or difficult as he had imagined it would be. His concern for the fossil's safety made him forget his own. Because of this he moved nimbly and fearlessly.

Within a couple of minutes—although they seemed to him like hours—Henry Hollins was standing safely on the shingle at the foot of the cliff. Without even pausing to congratulate himself on his feat, he lifted the dinosaur fossil from out of its resting-place and set it down on the shingle. Then he untied his coat-sleeves, slipped on the coat, picked up the fossil, and set off in a jog-trot across the beach towards the cove and the road beyond.

At exactly the same time, Albert Hollins was striding along the top of the cliff, the coil of rope from the boot of his car slung around his neck. Mr Hollins tut-tutted under his breath as his missed his footing in disused, overgrown rabbit-holes. He contemplated the minutes that were slipping by—minutes that he knew could only serve to increase the awful build-up of traffic between the seaside and Staplewood.

Mrs Hollins had been known to observe, on frequent occasions, that her husband spent his nights *dreaming* about traffic jams. This was not altogether true, but he did seem to spend an awful lot of his daylight hours worrying about them.

Albert Hollins arrived, with his rope, at the exact spot at the top of the cliff which, he believed, was directly above the ledge where his son was marooned. He leant over and peered down. There was the ledge, sure enough. But where was Henry? Perhaps, thought Mr Hollins, it was not the right ledge? He peered down again. It *was* the right ledge, without a doubt. For there above it lay the broken kite, still fluttering bravely in an attempt to free its string from a sprig of cliff-side gorse. And so what had become of Henry?

"Henry!" shouted Mr Hollins, cupping his hands and calling over the cliff. "Hen—r*ee*!" he yelled again, and again received no answer, except for a scream from an overhead seagull hoping, perhaps, for another custard tart to be thrown its way.

"He's making a complete fool of me, is that boy," grumbled Albert Hollins to himself. "Sending me off on a fool's errand along the top of a cliff with an enormous length of rope. As if I hadn't got anything better to do—and with the traffic building up on the motorway. I shall speak *very* severely to a certain young man when I do set eyes on him!" Albert Hollins jerked the coil of rope into a more comfortable position around his shoulder and strode off, back the way he had come, towards the car.

Overhead, the seagull gave up all hope of tasting another custard tart that afternoon, gently flapped its wings, and swooped off over the sea.

Not a vehicle moved in the line of cars that stretched along the motorway ahead, as far as the eye could see. Albert Hollins let out a frustrated groan and jammed his thumb down on the horn, hard, three times. Cars ahead of him and behind him took up the call, and the motorway was filled with a great tooting and hooting and honking and beeping.

"Now, that *does* remind me of something," said Emily Hollins. "I must remember to sort out some old woollens for the Noise Abatement Society next week."

Albert Hollins asked with amazement, "What on earth will the Noise Abatement Society do with old woollens?"

"I'm sure they'll think of something," said Emily, comfortably.

"Perhaps they'll stick them in car horns to stop them making so much noise," said Henry.

"Shut up," said Albert, turning on his son. "I hope you realize that this is all your fault," he added.

"Sorry, Dad," said Henry.

"Humph," sniffed Mr Hollins.

"Yes, Henry, but *are* you sorry?" said his mother, joining in. "I did tell you *not* to wander away, *and* not to get wet, *and* to keep away from those cliffs. I can't keep on telling you everything twice—I do have more than enough to do. As it is, I shall have to sit up in bed tonight and finish addressing those envelopes."

"Oh, Lord," said Mr Hollins, "does that mean that the bedroom light will be on half the night?"

"I can't address envelopes in the dark, dear, can I?" Emily Hollins pointed out, and added, "Look out, I think we're moving at last."

Mr Hollins gave his entire attention to the road

ahead. He released his handbrake as the line of cars moved forward for about twenty metres, and then he reapplied his handbrake as the queue of traffic stopped again. Albert Hollins let out yet another exasperated sigh, and turned back again, once more, to confront Henry. "If it hadn't been for your dilly-dallying on that cliff, holding us up," he said severely, "I'd have been cruising into Staplewood now, putting my foot down on an empty road."

"Sorry, Dad," said Henry, for the umpteenth time that afternoon.

"So you should be," snapped back his father, turning away and staring stonily at the road ahead, drumming his fingers on the steering-wheel. Another thought occurred to him. "And that reminds me," he said, "what did you do with that thingy?"

"What thingy?" asked Henry, innocently.

"That whatchamacallit? That bit of old stone. That *thingy*! Where is it?"

"Do you mean that fossil?"

"You know very well what I mean—I mean that thing you were holding on that ledge. You haven't still got it, have you?

"No, Dad," said Henry.

"And a good job too," said Albert. "I'm sick of having my garden shed cluttered up with *thingys*."

"I think we're about to move again, dear," said Emily Hollins, giving her husband a gentle nudge and taking his attention away from Henry.

Albert Hollins turned back and surveyed the road ahead. Emily was right, the traffic in front *was* moving forward, slowly but regularly, and even picking up some speed.

"Thank goodness for small mercies," said Albert Hollins, putting his foot down on the accelerator.

In the back seat, it was Henry's turn to let out a sigh of relief. Although he had told his father the truth—well, *almost* the truth—when he had said he hadn't got the dinosaur's egg, it was a statement that would not stand up to a great deal of examination. For at that moment the fossil, although not in Henry's *actual* possession, was only a few feet away from where he was sitting. It was in the boot of the car, nestling under a couple of coats, where he had managed to hide it while his father was on the cliff-top.

As the Hollins' family car made snail-like progress in that long procession of vehicles heading back from the sea, the dinosaur's egg went too, getting nearer and nearer to Staplewood where its presence, in the months to come, was to cause such chaos.

# 3

*Dinosaur remains were first discovered in America, over one hundred and fifty years ago, in the form of gigantic footprints. Some time later, the first dinosaur fossilized bones were uncovered and, gradually, as man fitted the bones together, he came to understand what these huge reptiles had looked like.*

*The word dinosaur comes from two Greek words:* deinos *and* saurus. *Deinos means terrible and* saurus *means lizard. For when the first dinosaur fossils were discovered and put together, they looked like the remains of enormous lizards, which was why they were given the name: Terrible Lizards . . .*

Henry Hollins turned over the page in his book of prehistoric reptiles, and reached across the breakfast table for another slice of toast from the toastrack. He already *knew* that dinosaur meant Terrible Lizard—it seemed that every book he read contained a long passage that told how the dinosaur came by its name—but he could not find one sentence in any of his books that told him anything at all about browny-grey fossilized dinosaur eggs.

"In any case," said Henry to himself, "it doesn't seem fair, calling them Terrible Lizards, when they weren't lizards at all, and most of them weren't very terrible—except to look at."

It was true that many of the dinosaurs had been harmless vegetarians that were too clumsy and weak to defend themselves from their enemies. The enormous *Brachiosaurus*, for example, which weighed all of fifty tons, was a plant-eating dinosaur that spent most of its life skulking in rivers; partly because it was so heavy that its legs could hardly support it on dry land, and partly because its brain was so small that it couldn't think quickly enough to help it escape from its attackers.

"*And* the *Diplodocus and* the *Brontosaurus and* the *Stegosaurus*," thought Henry, "they were all plant-eaters, so why should they be called terrible?"

Henry turned over a page with one hand and reached across the table for the butter dish with his other, knocking over the marmalade jar in the process.

"Look what you're doing, you clumsy idiot!" growled his father.

"Sorry, Dad," said Henry out loud and then, under his breath, he muttered, "*Deinos Daddius*—Terrible Father."

"What was that?" asked Albert Hollins, suspiciously.

"I said, 'sorry, Dad'," said Henry.

"I meant after that," said Albert Hollins. "What was that you muttered under your breath?"

36

"Nothing, Dad," said Henry, innocently. "I was just reading something out of this dinosaur book."

"How many times do you have to be told about reading at the table?" said Albert Hollins, over the top of his newspaper. "And isn't it about time you were getting yourself ready for school? It's well past eight o'clock, you know."

"No school today, Dad," said Henry. "It's half-term."

"It's *always* half-term," observed his father, gloomily. "And when you are at school, it's always either football or drama club. Don't you *ever* do *any* work?"

"I'm going to be a shepherd in this year's Nativity Play," said Henry.

"That's *just* what I'm getting at," said Albert, "you're rehearsing the Christmas play already and it isn't even July yet!"

Their conversation was interrupted by Emily, as she breezed in from the kitchen with her arms full of empty jam-jars. "I'm collecting these for the Society For Retired Greyhounds," she said. "Haven't I got a lot!"

"What possible use will the retired greyhounds find for an armful of jam-jars?" asked Albert, blinking hard with astonishment. "What do you imagine they'll *do* with them?"

Emily shrugged. "The same thing they did with the milk-bottle tops I sent them, I suppose," she said. "Anyway, I'm sure they'll think of something useful."

Then, deciding it was time to change the subject, she said, "Isn't it time you were setting off for work, Albert?"

Albert glanced up at the clock on the wall, pulled a face, folded his newspaper and got to his feet. "I suppose I ought to be making a move," he said. "There's always a dreadful traffic build-up on Monday mornings at that road junction coming out of Copperfield Street."

"Have a nice day, dear," said Emily as her husband moved towards the door. "Don't work *too* hard—enjoy yourself."

"Humph," said Albert Hollins, without much enthusiasm. He never worked harder than was necessary, and he couldn't remember when he had last *enjoyed* himself at his place of work.

Albert Hollins worked in the office of a factory that made plaster ornaments of geese-in-flight; plaster garden gnomes; and—a recent addition to the factory's output—small plaster busts of Charles Dickens which were proving a very popular line in the Common Market countries and also in certain areas of Japan.

Albert Hollins paused at the door of the dining-room and gazed, balefully, at his only son. Mr Hollins was envious of the fact that while he was going to spend his day sitting at a desk in a stuffy office, writing boring letters about busts of Charles Dickens, and posting them off to boring people all over

Europe—to say nothing of certain areas of Japan—his son could spend the whole of the day doing just whatever took his fancy.

"By the way, Henry," said Albert Hollins in ominous tones.

"Yes, Dad?" said Henry, glancing up in some surprise and accidentally knocking over the milk jug.

"Be so good as to keep out of my garden shed," said his father. "I'm fed up to the back teeth with you cluttering up my shed with bits of bone and old rocks."

"All right, Dad," said Henry.

"And *try* and keep out of mischief," his father went on. "I don't want to pick up my *Staplewood Guardian* tonight and read that you've blown up the Electricity Showrooms or robbed the Bingo Hall. Understood?"

"Loud and clear," said Henry.

"Over and out," said Mr Hollins. The door slammed behind him.


The editor-in-chief of the *Staplewood Guardian* glanced over the top of his glasses and glared at his junior reporter, his moustache bristling. "What I want," he said, "is a news story that is different."

"Yes, sir," said the junior reporter, taking out his pocket diary and flicking nervously through its pages. "Well, sir," he went on, "there's a meeting of the Friends of Charles Dickens Society in the Pump

Room of the Pig and Bucket at 7 p.m. on Tuesday evening . . ."

"There's a meeting of the Friends of Charles Dickens Society *every* Tuesday evening," growled the editor-in-chief.

"No, sir, not quite," said the junior reporter, "it's every second Tuesday in the month."

"Don't argue," said the editor-in-chief. "What else is on?"

The junior reporter flicked through more pages, aimlessly. "Well, sir," he said at last, "I could go out to the plaster ornaments factory again."

"What for?" said the editor-in-chief.

The junior reporter shrugged. "I could take a photographer out there," he said. "He could take some very interesting photographs of men making plaster gnomes and geese-in-flight."

"I am sick and tired of seeing photographs in my paper of men making plaster gnomes," thundered the editor-in-chief, and he continued: "And if I see just one more picture of a plaster goose-in-flight in my middle pages, I shall scream. Do I make myself clear?"

"Yes, sir," said the junior reporter, sadly.

"Now get out into those streets and don't come back until you've got a story. Something that is different! Something that is news!"

The junior reporter looked out of the window and shuffled his feet. "Sir?" he said.

"What is it now?"

"It's raining."

The editor-in-chief's face began to turn purple and the junior reporter shot out through the door. He decided that he would be better off in the rainy streets of Staplewood than he was in the presence of a purple editor-in-chief.

Henry Hollins came out through the double swing doors of the Staplewood public library. He paused at the top of the white, worn steps that led down into the High Street. He looked up at the dull, grey skies and the pouring rain, turned up his coat collar, and shifted the weight of the dinosaur fossil from one arm to the other.

Henry had just spent a fruitless half-hour in the Natural History section of the library, looking for information about dinosaur eggs. In one book, he had read about the huge *Antrodemus* that had a mouth so big it could swallow quite large reptiles whole; and in another book he had read about the *Styracosaurus*, which had a beak like a parrot and big spikes on top of its head. But Henry had known about these creatures before. He had found nothing new about dinosaur eggs. He *had* discovered a rather interesting-looking book on the top shelf that he had not seen before. He had been just about to take it down from off the shelf when he had felt a tap on his shoulder.

Henry had turned to find himself looking up at a peaked cap, from beneath which there frowned the stern face of the library's uniformed attendant.

"Is that your grey stone thing?" the attendant had said, pointing at the dinosaur egg that Henry had left unattended on the library table.

"It's not a grey stone thing," Henry had said. "It's a fossil."

"I don't care what it is," the official had snapped. "We don't allow umbrellas, pets or parcels to be left lying about the library."

"It's not an umbrella or a pet," Henry had replied, "and it's not a parcel either."

"Ah!" the library attendant had countered, "it's only *not* a parcel because it hasn't got brown paper and string round it—it's a parcel in every other respect. And it's near enough a parcel to be not allowed in this library. Kindly remove it."

"But—" began Henry.

"You heard. I said 'out'," said the uniformed official. "And take that grey stone unwrapped parcel thing with you!"

And Henry, with a sigh, had picked up his dinosaur fossil and left.

Sheltering from the rain on the library steps, he found himself joined by a young man who was wearing a large trilby hat and who was carrying a sodden shorthand notebook.

The junior reporter from the *Staplewood Guardian*

had also suffered a rather unsuccessful morning. Having left the *Guardian* offices, he had first hung about outside the fire station for half an hour, in the hope that the Staplewood fire brigade might have been called out. But there had not been so much as a false alarm or a summons to douse a smouldering fish-shop chip pan. Giving up in disgust, the junior reporter had next taken himself to the Pig and Bucket, in the faint hope that there might be something newsworthy happening in the famous Charles Dickens' bedroom. But there was nothing exciting going on there—in fact, there was nothing happening there at all, except for a couple of tourists peering around. They were accompanied by their small son who, bored, was picking his nose and standing on one leg. The junior reporter had moved on to the Bleak House Café, where he had taken his morning coffee break. His final port of call had been the porch of the public library where he now stood, sheltering from the rain.

The junior reporter took off his trilby hat and shook it, vigorously. A myriad drops of rain flew off, spraying the library porch, some of them falling on to a boy who was also sheltering from the rain, holding a large smooth browny-grey object.

"Sorry about that," said the junior reporter.

"That's all right," said Henry Hollins.

The junior reporter put his trilby back on his head and turned his attention to the rain-soaked pages of

44

his shorthand notebook. He flicked through them, but found nothing written there except on one page where it said:

TO EXPENSES:
BLEAK HOUSE CAFÉ, ONE CUP COFFEE . . . 15 PENCE

The junior reporter sighed and snapped shut his notebook. He was not even sure that he would be able to claim his coffee money, on a morning when he had failed to find any news worth writing about. There was only one thing for it, he decided. He would have to catch a bus out to the plaster ornament factory and write a human interest story about garden gnomes and the men who made them. Or possibly about plaster geese-in-flight? But he dismissed both ideas as quickly as they came into his mind. Neither of them, he knew, would satisfy his editor-in-chief. He glanced down again at the boy who was sharing the porch with him. His eyes strayed to the browny-grey object that was tucked underneath the boy's arm.

"That looks rather interesting," said the junior reporter, hopefully.

"Yes," said Henry Hollins, and added: "It's a dinosaur fossil."

The junior reporter looked puzzled. He knew very little about Natural History and nothing at all about fossils. "Oh yes?" he said. "Has it got anything to do with Charles Dickens?"

"No, nothing," said Henry Hollins.

"Oh," said the junior reporter, a shade despondently.

"It's a fossilized egg," Henry Hollins went on to explain. "It's over two hundred million years old."

"Is that a fact?" said the junior reporter, his interest perking up. "Two hundred million years ago? That's before Charles Dickens was even *born*, isn't it?"

"Oh, yes," said Henry Hollins. "Long before."

"Who does it belong to?" asked the junior reporter.

"It's mine. I found it," said Henry Hollins.

The junior reporter flicked open his notebook again and found a page that was dry enough to write on. "And what's your name?" he said. "And where do you come from?"

"Henry Hollins," said Henry Hollins. "And I live here."

"*Here?*" The junior reporter sounded overjoyed. "In Staplewood? You're a local resident then? Wow! This is a *local* news story!"

"Is that good?" asked Henry.

"Terrific!" replied the junior reporter. "Would you mind very much coming along to the *Guardian* offices and letting one of our photographers take a picture of your what-do-you-call-it? Fissol?"

"Not at all," said Henry, and he added: "It's a dinosaur fossil."

Angus McGillicuddy, the chief photographer of the *Staplewood Guardian,* prowled round the dinosaur fossil, which was perched on top of a filing cabinet. Henry Hollins and the junior reporter watched Mr McGillicuddy and said nothing, as he pulled faces and muttered to himself under his breath. At last, he spoke aloud.

"Are you wanting a picture of yon thing for tonight's edition, then?" he said.

"That's right, Mr McGillicuddy," said the junior reporter.

"Oh, aye?" said the chief photographer. "And whereabouts in tonight's paper were you reckoning on putting it?"

"On the front page, of course," said the junior reporter. "It's over two hundred million years old. It's . . . a . . . It's . . . a . . . fissol."

"It's a dinosaur fossil—a fossilized egg," said Henry, helpfully.

"That's right," said the junior reporter. "And this lad found it, he's a local resident. It's local news. It's a front-page story."

"Is it indeed?" said Angus McGillicuddy. "And tell me now, does the editor-in-chief know what you've got in store for his front page this evening?"

"Not yet," said the junior reporter, with quiet pride. "It's going to be a surprise for him."

"Humph," said Angus McGillicuddy, and he

walked slowly round the fossil once again, scowling and muttering to himself.

"Is anything the matter?" asked Henry Hollins.

"Aye," said the chief photographer, "there's a great deal the matter; it's nae topical, for one thing, and it's a' a question of relativity for another. D'ye ken?"

"No," said Henry, "I don't ken—sorry—I mean, I don't understand."

"Why, it's simple, laddie," said Mr McGillicuddy. "If it was Easter, say, I could take a picture of yon thing standing next to an Easter egg. Now, that would make the picture topical. And it would also give the newspaper reader an idea of the size of yon thing, judging it by the Easter egg—and that's what I mean by relativity. Or, if it was hogmanay, I could photograph yon thing standing proudly alongside a haggis. Now, d'ye ken?"

"No," said Henry. "What's hogmanay?"

Mr McGillicuddy snorted peevishly. "Hoots mon!" he said.

"Hogmanay," said the junior reporter quickly, "is what Scottish people call New Year's Eve. Right, Mr McGillicuddy?"

"Nae! It's nae right!" stormed Mr McGillicuddy, getting more and more Scottish by the second. "New Year's Eve is what you Sassenachs call hogmanay!"

"What's a Sassenach?" asked Henry, innocently.

Mr McGillicuddy snorted and blew out through his nostrils, like an old cart horse.

"Let's not go into all that now," the junior reporter put in hastily. "Look, Mr McGillicuddy," he continued. "You're wrong about this—this what-do-you-call it . . . ?"

"Fossil," said Henry obligingly.

"Thank you," said the junior reporter. "You're wrong about this fissol not being topical. Henry only found it yesterday, so that makes it up to date. And if you want something to judge it by its size in the photograph—why don't you photograph Henry holding it. He lives in Staplewood, and that's why it's a local-interest news story."

The chief photographer was forced to admit that the junior reporter had a good point. In no time at all, Henry was standing on top on the filing cabinet, holding aloft the dinosaur fossil.

"Smile, please, laddie. Say cheese," said the chief photographer.

"Gorgonzola," said Henry, and he gave a broad smile.

At that precise moment, the editor-in-chief swept through the office. He glared at the junior reporter. Then he glared up at Henry on the filing cabinet. Then he glared down again at the junior reporter. "What is that boy doing up on that filing cabinet?" he demanded. "And why aren't you out scouring the streets of Staplewood for a story?"

"I've got one, sir!" said the junior reporter. "And that boy is it—at least, that thing he's holding in his hands is news."

"What is it?" muttered the editor-in-chief, suspiciously.

The junior reporter thought hard. "It's . . . a . . . It's . . . a . . . fissol."

"It's a fossilized dinosaur egg," said Henry, from his perch on top of the filing cabinet.

"That's right, sir," said the junior reporter, and the words began to fairly bubble out of him. "It's a fissolized dinosaur's egg, sir. It's over two hundred million years old. He found it. His name is Henry Hollins and he lives right here in Staplewood. It's a front-page story."

The editor-in-chief gave his junior reporter a sour look over the top of his glasses. "A fossil", he said, "is not news—it's ancient history." And then he turned his gaze on Henry. "Get down from there, lad," he said. "Your shoes are making scuff marks all over the paintwork on that filing cabinet." Then the editor-in-chief strode on, through the maze of desks, into his private office.

Sadly, Henry clambered to the ground.

# 4

*King Arthur drew Excalibur from its jewelled scabbard with a broad flourish and then pointed to a distant mountain. "Brabadush abadush oshky poshky!" proclaimed the monarch of all England.*

*"Oshky poshky?" replied Sir Bedivere.*

*"Oshky poshky brabadush abadush dushibush pushibush," said Sir Lancelot, raising his burnished shield on high.*

Henry Hollins let out a small exasperated sigh. He was watching Episode Five of a six-part serial about Camelot on the TV in the living-room of his home. The serial had been made in a foreign language in a country somewhere in the middle of Europe. It had been given English subtitles, but for some unknown reason, the words never seemed to quite fit into the bottom of the Hollins' TV screen. Henry had seen all five of the episodes so far, but he was still not sure what it was all about.

*King Arthur, Sir Bedivere and Sir Lancelot reined in their richly canopied chargers, dismounted, and paused to look down an ancient, crumbling well. Sir Bedivere dropped a stone down the well and, seconds later, the sound of the splash echoed up.*

"*Abadush brabadush pushibush abadush?*" *said Sir Bedivere, apparently in some surprise.*

"*Pushibush brabadush poshky oshky?*" *said Sir Lancelot.*

"*Oshky poshky pushky pash!*" *cried King Arthur, again whipping out Excalibur and waving it above his head.*

"Do we *have* to put up with that?" asked Albert Hollins, coming in from the dining-room with a copy of the *Staplewood Guardian* under his arm. "I've been sitting writing letters to foreigners all day—I don't expect to have to come home and listen to them on the box."

"They're not supposed to *be* foreigners," said Henry. "They're supposed to be King Arthur and his Knights."

"Don't argue with your father, Henry," said Emily, who was sitting in a corner of the living-room, quietly knitting dish-cloths for a tribe of deprived pygmies somewhere in Central Africa. "Your father has had a hard day at the office. He wants to read his newspaper in peace. Switch off the television, dear. If you're looking for something to do, you can help me by sorting out some soup-tin labels I've tipped out on the bedroom floor."

"How many soup-tin labels are there?" asked Henry.

"Three thousand five hundred," said his mother.

"No, thanks," said Henry.

Albert Hollins sat bolt upright in his chair. "*Three*

*thousand* five hundred soup-tin labels?" he thundered. "All over my bedroom?"

"Yes, dear," said Emily. "For every two thousand labels you collect, the manufacturers are going to provide bamboo shoots for a whole family of panda bears in a Dublin Zoo—it's Animal Year, apparently, in Ireland."

"I give up," muttered Albert Hollins, and he hid himself behind his newspaper.

While this conversation had been going on, Henry had crossed the room and taken a book about dinosaurs out of the bookshelf. He was now sitting back in his chair, turning over pages and looking for a chapter about dinosaur eggs.

Albert Hollins appeared again, out from behind his newspaper. "Hello!" he said, and, "Well, I never!" and then, "I've only just noticed—they have done us proud tonight!"

"What's that, dear?" asked his wife, and then she frowned as she held up a dish-cloth and examined it. "Do you think they'll *know* these are dish-cloths, those pygmies? Or will they mistake them for loin-cloths?"

"Does it matter, just so long as they find *some* use for them?" said Albert, rather testily. "And are you interested in what I was saying, or aren't you?"

"Of course I am, Albert," said Emily. "Do tell me."

Albert Hollins rustled his newspaper importantly, hoping also to draw Henry's attention before he spoke. "There's a photograph, right across the front page, of one of our workmen at the factory making a plaster gnome! It's a bit blurred—I can't tell whether it's Harry Armitage or Cyril Witherspoon."

"I didn't know that plaster gnomes had got names?" said Emily Hollins.

"I don't *mean* the gnome—I mean the workman," said Albert, giving his wife a sour glance, and then he went on: "It says 'A Staplewood Craftsman' above the picture, and then underneath it goes on to say that the factory is one of the biggest exporters of garden gnomes in the whole country!"

"Very good, Albert," said Emily. "Did you hear that, Henry?"

"Yes, Mum," said Henry, and he turned over another page in his dinosaur book, and began to read:

*The* Oviraptor *was a sly and cunning dinosaur that lived on earth one hundred million years ago.* Oviraptor *means Egg Stealer, for the* Oviraptor *lived on the eggs he stole from the nests of other dinosaurs.* "Ah-hah," thought Henry, "now we're getting somewhere at last!" And he read on: *One of* Oviraptor's *favourite victims was* Protoceratops *who often returned to her nest to find it had been plundered by this clever but toothless enemy.* Protoceratops, *which means horn-faced lizard, was a dinosaur that grew to about two metres in length, and looked much fiercer than it really was, for* Protoceratops *was another plant-eating dinosaur . . .*

"I don't believe it!" Henry looked up from his book

54

as his father's surprised voice broke in on his thoughts. "I just don't believe it!" said Albert Hollins for the second time.

"What don't you believe, Albert?" asked Emily, her needles clicking furiously as she knitted away at a second dish-cloth for some lucky pygmy.

"Our Henry. He's in here!"

"Yes, dear, of course he is," said Emily, rather puzzled, and she pointed across the room. "He's sitting in that corner, reading a book."

"No, no, no!" said Albert, prodding at his newspaper with his forefinger. "I mean in *here*. He's got himself in the newspaper."

"Have I?" said Henry, in some surprise.

"Perhaps it's another Henry Hollins, Albert," said Emily.

"No, it's him all right," said Albert. "It's got our name and address as well: Woodview, 23 Nicholas Nickleby Close—that's *here*."

"Oh dear me," said Emily, "what *has* he been up to now?"

"I tell you," began Albert, glowering across the room at Henry, "he has one day off school and he gets himself plastered all over the *Staplewood Guardian!* He's not fit to be trusted out on his own."

Emily Hollins "tut-tutted" and cast Henry a worried frown. "You'd better read it out, Albert, and tell us the worst," she said.

Albert Hollins cleared his throat, twice, and read

aloud from the newspaper: "'Staplewood Boy Finds Fissol'." Albert turned to Henry, puzzled. "What's a fissol?" he asked.

"I think it's meant to be fossil," said Henry. "The reporter who interviewed me about it never could seem to get it right."

Albert shook his head, slowly, and then: "I don't know," he said, as if the mis-spelling was Henry's fault too. "'Staplewood Boy Finds Fissol'," Albert began again. "Henry Hollins, a local boy, who lives at Woodview, 23 Nicholas Nickleby Close, found a dinosaur fissol while spending a day by the sea with his parents—"

"Oh?" said Emily, perking up. "We get a mention as well, do we?"

". . . while spending a day by the sea with his parents at Gunnersby Cove yesterday," continued Albert, frowning at his wife for her interruption. "The fissol is believed to be over two hundred million years old and is thought to be an egg of some kind."

"Is that *all* it says?" asked Emily, disappointed.

"That's all," said Albert.

"Well," said Emily, "you'd have thought they might have given my door-to-door campaign on behalf of the Wild Flowers of the Woodland a mention at least!"

Albert's attention was turned on Henry. "And where is this fissol or follis or whatever it is you call it?" he asked.

"I've put it away."

"Away where?"

Henry shrugged. "Somewhere safe," he said.

"And where's somewhere safe?"

"Er . . ." Henry scratched his head and put his tongue in his cheek as though deep in thought. He was playing for time, but he knew that the end was not now far away.

"Well?" said Albert. "Come on, Henry—I'm waiting."

"It's in the garden shed," said Henry, resignedly.

"*My* garden shed?"

"Mmmm."

"I thought I told you, my lad, to clear your things *out* of my garden shed, not put any more of your rubbish into it." Albert, exasperated, flung his *Staplewood Guardian* to the floor, rose to his feet and walked round the room slowly, casting occasional sly glances at Henry, like a hungry beast stalking its cowering prey.

"*Deinos Daddius*," muttered Henry, for the second time that day, but this time he made quite sure that his father didn't hear him.

Albert Hollins pulled up short, struck by a sudden thought. "Just a minute," he said. "This thingy you found? It's not the same thingy I saw you messing about with half-way up that cliff, is it?"

"Er . . . yes, Dad."

"I thought I told you to throw it away yesterday? In

57

fact, as I remember, you *told* me you *had* thrown it away."

"I thought I had done," said Henry, unconvincingly. "I must have forgot."

"And all the time you were lying," went on Albert, paying no attention to his son's words. "Well, you can just take yourself down that garden, now, and bring that thingy to me. Because *I'm* going to throw it away—personally—myself—and when I throw things away they remain thrown."

"But, Dad—"

"You heard," said Albert, firmly. "Bring it here. And I'm putting it straight in the dustbin."

"But, Dad—"

"No 'buts'," said Albert, firmly. "Fetch it here now—or else . . . ! *Scoot!*"

Henry Hollins scooted.


Morning came to Nicholas Nickleby Close with the merry clatter of galvanized dustbins. Albert Hollins stood by the front door of Number 23 and smiled to himself. He watched the dustbin man carry the full dustbin down the garden path. His smile widened as he saw the contents of the dustbin tumbling out into the dustcart, and that same broadening smile stretched into a grin as he saw the browny-grey egg-shaped thingy fall out of the dustbin, among a jumble of cornflake packets and potato peelings, and fumble and rumble closer towards the huge mechanized jaws.

Mr Hollins was whistling a jolly tune to himself as he walked into the dining-room. "By the way," he said, giving Emily a cheerful wink, "I think I've cracked that traffic bottle-neck build-up near Copperfield Street."

"Oh?" said Mrs Hollins, busy at the table with the morning toast. "That just reminds me—I must remember to put out all those empty Tizer bottles for the Boy Scouts to take away in Bob-a-Job Week."

Mr Hollins chose to ignore his wife's latest good deed. "Yes," he continued, rubbing his hands together briskly, "I found a back-double yesterday morning." He glanced over at Henry who was picking at the contents of his cereal bowl. "Cheer up, Dismal Desmond. It was only a piece of old rock, cluttering up the garden shed."

"It wasn't a piece of old rock," said Henry. "It was a very rare fossil."

"Worse things happen at sea, don't they, dear?" he said to his wife.

"Indeed they do," said Mrs Hollins. "That's why we must all remember to dig deep into our purses or pockets on Lifeboat Day."

At which point, the telephone rang in the hall. "I'll get it," said Albert and, still whistling to himself, he walked out of the room and picked up the phone. "Hello? This is Staplewood 65237," he said and, still feeling rather perky, continued, "the Hollins abode—which one of the Hollinses would you like to speak to?"

"Is that Mr *Albert* Hollins?" asked a rather posh voice.

"It is indeed," said Albert. "Albert Hollins, at your service!"

"Ah! Good morrow, Mr Hollins," said the rather posh voice. "This is the BBC this end!"

Albert Hollins frowned, pursed his lips, took the telephone away from his ear and looked into the mouthpiece suspiciously. People had been known to play tricks on him before. He wasn't going to fall for one of them again. "Is this one of our Henry's pals?" he asked, and added, "larking about, trying to be funny?"

"Really, Mr Hollins, I can assure you that I *never* lark about. I leave all that kind of thing to the Light Entertainment Department."

"Do you mean to say that you really *are* the BBC?" asked an astonished Albert.

"I am indeed," said the posh voice. "My name is Julian Derwent-Smith, and I am the producer of the *Half-Past-Six Show!* You've probably seen it. It goes out at half-past six!"

"No, I don't think I have," said Albert.

"Oh, I'm sure you must have done," said Mr Derwent-Smith. "It's a features programme. We interview people who are in the news."

"Is it that programme that goes out when there's a cowboy programme on the other channel?" asked Albert Hollins.

There was a pause, and then Julian Derwent-Smith replied, rather huffily, "Yes, it is."

"Ah," said Albert Hollins, "then I don't think I have seen it. I always watch the cowboy programme."

"Hmmm," said Julian Derwent-Smith. "To each his own."

"Anyway, what can I do for you, Mr Smith?" asked Albert Hollins.

"*Derwent*-Smith," said Julian Derwent-Smith, "and I'm really ringing up about your son."

"Our Henry?" said Albert. "Go on—tell me the bad news—what's he done now? Set fire to Broadcasting House or something?"

"Why, no," said Julian Derwent-Smith. "Isn't he the boy who found the dinosaur fossil?"

"Oh that," said Albert. "How did you come to hear about it?"

"We follow up quite a number of things in the local papers," said Mr Derwent-Smith. "And this fossil find sounds rather interesting. We wondered if you'd care to bring along your son to the studios this evening? For an interview."

"*Me?*" said Albert Hollins, very impressed. "Come to the BBC?"

"If it's no trouble," said Mr Derwent-Smith. "We'll

send round one of our BBC chauffeur-driven cars to bring you to the studio."

"Crikey!" said Albert Hollins, and: "Well I never!"

About five minutes later, the door to the dining-room opened and Albert walked in, trying to look casual.

"You were a long time on that telephone," said Emily. "Who was it?"

"You'll never guess," said Albert, hugging his secret to himself. "Go on, try—you as well, Henry—see if you can guess who it was."

"Oh, I haven't got time for guessing games, Albert," said Emily Hollins. "Anyway, all the toast has gone cold while you were out. I'll have to do some more."

"Come on," urged Albert. "You can have twenty questions—and I bet you still won't guess who it was."

"All right then," said Emily Hollins, entering into the spirit of things. "Was it Animal, Vegetable or Mineral?"

"Don't be daft, Emily," said Albert. "It must have been animal, mustn't it? Ringing up. It couldn't have been vegetable, could it? I mean, you'd hardly expect a whopping great cabbage or a giant cauliflower to come on to the telephone."

"I wouldn't expect a kangaroo neither, nor a hippopotamus," said Emily Hollins, "but you said it was animal. Who was it, then? I give up."

"It was the BBC," said Albert proudly.

"The BBC *isn't* animal, is it, Dad?" said Henry. "It's mineral, it's made of stone and metal."

"Aye, aye," said Albert Hollins. "Hark at clever-clogs. All right, Mr Funny-One, I meant it was a *person* at the BBC. It was a Mr Julian Derwent-Smith."

"Oh," said Emily, "that just reminds me—I must remember to send off some old socks for those seaside donkeys that children's programme is collecting for."

Albert resisted the temptation to ask what seaside donkeys could do with old socks. He was too full of his own news.

"He wants me to take our Henry round there this evening to be interviewed. About that fossil thingy."

"What?" exclaimed Emily. "Our Henry? On the telly?"

"Yes," said Albert. "On that programme that goes out while the cowboy programme we always watch is on."

"It's called *The Half-Past-Six Show!*" said Henry.

"That's right," said Albert, and he drew himself up, importantly, before imparting his last piece of news. "They're sending round a chauffeur-driven car to take us to the studio."

"Well!" said Emily. "Whatever next?"

"It's coming here at five o'clock to pick us up. It's cutting things a bit fine, but I've promised to show the driver the back-doubles round Copperfield Street. I

shall need a clean shirt, of course, and if you do have a minute you might just run an iron over my best trousers."

"I thought it was our Henry that was being interviewed, not you," said Emily.

Albert Hollins chose to ignore his wife's sarcasm, and turned to Henry. "And see that you look neat and tidy too, my lad. And get that fossil thingy polished up."

"I can't," said Henry. "You threw it in the dustbin."

"Good Lord!" cried Albert Hollins, for in his excitement over the telephone call, he had quite forgotten what had happened to the dinosaur fossil. "The dustbin men have got it as well!" he said. Albert Hollins ran from the room.

The Staplewood dustcart was pulling out of Nicholas Nickleby Close and cruising into Chuzzlewit Gardens when Albert Hollins, still in his woolly plaid dressing-gown, rushed out of Woodview.

"Wait! Wait!" he cried, and: "Stop! Stop!"

But the dustcart turned the corner and disappeared from sight. Albert Hollins set off in pursuit of the corporation dustcart, running as fast as he could, his slippers flip-flapping on the pavement.

# 5

Albert Hollins leant forward and put his thumb on the switch. The window between the driver's compartment and the passenger seats in the big, black limousine slid down without a sound.

"If I were you," observed Albert to the uniformed BBC chauffeur, "I'd turn off the motorway at the next junction, then take the bypass road rather than go on to the dual carriageway into the centre of the city."

"That would be going the long way round." The chauffeur spoke without turning his head.

"Ah!" said Albert, triumphantly. "It's a longer journey—yes. But I think you'll find there's a lot less traffic."

"Humph," said the BBC chauffeur, "that's as maybe—but I think I'll risk the dual carriageway."

"You're the driver," said Albert, "but I was only trying to help." He pressed the switch again and this time the window slid up. Albert Hollins looked across at Henry who was sitting at his side, with the dinosaur fossil nestling safely in his lap. "You ought to be very grateful to me, Henry," said Albert. "If I hadn't dashed down the street in my dressing-gown, you might never have set eyes on that thingy again."

"Thanks very much," said Henry.

"I had to crawl right into the back of that dustcart to get it out, snatching it out from the jaws of death, risking life and limb—*and* getting old potato-peelings in my dressing-gown pocket. You ought to be *very* grateful indeed."

"It *was* you that threw it into the dustbin in the first place," Henry pointed out.

"Yes, well . . ." said Albert, shuffling his feet on the thick carpet on the floor of the limousine, ". . . we can all make mistakes, can't we?"

Henry did not reply, and the journey to the television studios continued in silence.

Julian Derwent-Smith came down in person to meet Albert and Henry when they arrived at the television studios. He was a short, tubby man who waved his arms a lot whenever he spoke. "Welcome! Welcome!" he said, as he breezed up to greet them at the reception desk. "My word, you got here in jolly good time!"

"Yes," said Albert, "but we might have got here even quicker, if your driver had taken my advice and come down the bypass—there was a queue of traffic five miles long on that dual carriageway."

"Not to worry," said Julian Derwent-Smith. "You've got lots of time for a spot of refreshment before we go on the air. Come with me. So *that's* what a dinosaur fossil looks like, eh?" And still talking ninety to the dozen, and waving his arms in the air,

Mr Derwent-Smith led the way down a long corridor, round a corner and then down an even longer corridor at the end of which was a door that was marked: Hospitality Room.

"Do come in, gentlemen," said Mr Derwent-Smith, flinging open the door.

Inside the Hospitality Room was a table on which were bottles containing all kinds of drinks, and some plates containing different sorts of sandwiches. A small lady in a flowered hat was helping herself to a selection of sandwiches as Julian Derwent-Smith, Henry and Albert Hollins walked into the room.

"Making yourself at home, Mrs Murchison?" said Julian Derwent-Smith. "Jolly good!"

"Aaah-choo!" said the lady called Mrs Murchison.

"Mrs Murchison is another guest on our programme this evening," explained Mr Derwent-Smith to Henry and Albert. "She's with us because she hasn't stopped sneezing for over a fortnight, have you, Mrs Murchison?"

"Aaah-choo!" went Mrs Murchison.

"How do you do, Mrs Murchison?" said Albert Hollins.

"Aaah-choo!" was the only reply he got.

"Jolly good," said Julian Derwent-Smith, happily. "I think we've got the makings of a *really* interesting programme tonight. Well, I'll leave you lovely people to get to know each other, if I may, while I go and see how things are getting on in the control box. I'll be

68

back to take you all along to the studio, ready for the programme, in about quarter of an hour." Julian Derwent-Smith gave a cheery wave of his hand as he made for the door, where he paused. "Oh, by the way," he said, "we're hoping that Professor Corrigan will be coming along to join us—he's an expert on fossils, you know." With which, Mr Derwent-Smith left the room.

"Sandwich, Henry?" asked Albert Hollins.

Henry shook his head. "No, thanks, Dad," he said. Henry was already getting butterflies in his tummy at the thought of the impending television appearance. "I'll have something after the programme," he said.

"You want to dig in now while it's there, son," advised his father. "There might not *be* anything after the programme—they might clear this lot away while we're out of the room. What do you think, Mrs Murchison?"

"Aaah-choo!" she sneezed.

Albert Hollins took a plate from off the table and held it up for Henry to see. "It's got BBC written round the edge," he said. "They make sure nobody pinches the crockery, don't they?" And then he helped himself to three sardine-and-tomato sandwiches and one cheese-and-lettuce one. He also took a raspberry bun from a plate of cakes. "I don't suppose you've seen any custard tarts knocking about anywhere, have you?" he asked Mrs Murchison.

"Aaah-choo!" replied Mrs Murchison, who was also helping herself to more sandwiches.

"She might not be able to speak for sneezing," thought Henry to himself, "but it certainly doesn't stop her eating." And he sat back, the dinosaur egg on his lap, and watched his father and Mrs Murchison demolishing the grub.

True to his word, Julian Derwent-Smith came back a quarter of an hour later. He popped his head into the Hospitality Room, gave the three occupants another cheery wave of his hand, and said, "Well then, are we all fit?"

"Aaah-choo!" went Mrs Murchison.

"Jolly good," said Mr Derwent-Smith. "We're on the air in ten minutes from now. I'll take you along to Studio Two."

Henry and Albert Hollins and Mrs Murchison followed Julian Derwent-Smith through a maze of corridors, passing dressing-rooms, make-up rooms, workshops, and through lofty scene-docks, smelling of paint and glue, where props and settings for all kinds of plays and programmes were stacked in seemingly endless rows.

"Almost there now," said Julian Derwent-Smith, as they walked down yet another long corridor. "I'll drop Henry and Mrs Murchison in the studio, Mr Hollins, and then you can come up with me into the control box."

"Oh," said Albert, rather disappointed to hear that

he wasn't going to be allowed to sit in the studio while the programme was being televised.

"You'll like it in the control box, you'll see where all the *real* work is done."

"Oh?" said Albert Hollins, brightening slightly.

"I can't imagine what's happened to Professor Corrigan," Julian Derwent-Smith continued. "He should have been here half an hour ago—we look like having to go on the air without him."

"I should think he's probably got caught in traffic—if he's had to come along that dual carriageway," said Albert, and he added: "It's chock-a-block."

"More than likely," said Julian Derwent-Smith, as he opened a thick, soundproof door. "Here we are then, Studio Two. Jolly good."

The studio was dazzling with lights that seemed to shine down from everywhere. When Henry's eyes became accustomed to the glare, he saw that there were three cameras in the studio and that they were all turned towards a sort of dais on which there stood five or six swivel chairs. Behind the row of chairs there was a big, golden, glittering sign that said:

THE HALF-PAST-SIX SHOW!

As Henry stood taking all this in, with his father, Mrs Murchison and Mr Derwent-Smith, a youngish man wearing headphones and a worried expression came up to join them.

"Ah!" said Julian Derwent-Smith. "This is Tommy, our studio manager. Tommy, meet Mrs Murchison and Henry, our guests on the programme this evening."

"Hello," said Tommy.

"Hello," said Henry.

"Aaah-choo!" went Mrs Murchison.

"Jolly good," said Mr Derwent-Smith. "Well, it's high time I wasn't here," he continued. "Good luck, Mrs Murchison. Good luck, Henry. Don't be nervous—I *know* we're going to have a jolly interesting programme tonight." Then, taking Albert by the upper arm, he left the studio.

Tommy, the studio manager, glanced at the dinosaur fossil in Henry's hands. "What's that then, young feller-me-lad?" he asked.

"It's a fossilized dinosaur's egg," said Henry. "I'm here to be interviewed about it."

"Is it really?" said Tommy. "We get all kinds of things on this programme, you know. We had a man here last week who brought a tarantula spider in a cardboard box!" Then, turning to Mrs Murchison, he went on: "And what are you being interviewed about, Mrs Murchison?"

"Aaah-choo!" went Mrs Murchison.

Before the studio manager could make any reply to Mrs Murchison's sneeze, a message came through on his headphones and he paused and listened for several moments, and then said aloud to somebody who was not there, "All right, control, will do!" And then he turned and called out to the cameramen and studio technicians, "Three minutes to transmission, everybody—cut the cackle, please!" The studio manager turned next to Henry and Mrs Murchison. "Come on, you two," he said, "I'll show you where we're going to put you."

Tommy, the studio manager, led Henry and Mrs Murchison up on to the dais where a man with a bow-tie and a bald head had already taken his place in the middle of the row of swivel chairs, and was having his shiny forehead dabbed at by a make-up lady with a large powder puff.

"This is Norman Prendergast," said the studio manager, introducing Henry and Mrs Murchison to the man with the bow-tie. "He'll be interviewing you both."

"Do sit down, dears," said Norman Prendergast, giving them a wide smile and showing a lot of teeth. "I have been briefed about you both. You're the lady with the sneeze, and you're the young man with the fossil. Am I right?"

Mrs Murchison and Henry Hollins nodded their heads in unison.

"Thank heaven for that," Norman Prendergast continued, "I'm glad we've got you established before the start. Last week I got my cards mixed up and I introduced a cabinet minister as an ex-convict. He wasn't at *all* pleased!"

Just then, there was a slight kerfuffle by the studio door as a tall man with glasses and white spiky hair came in, making a clatter as he knocked over a sign that said: *Silence.*

"Professor Corrigan!" Norman Prendergast called out to the man as he untangled his legs from the sign and stood it back on its feet. "This way!"

The professor blinked owlishly through his glasses and made his way clumsily across to the dais, managing to trip over a camera cable *en route.* "Sorry I'm late," he said, as he stumbled up on to the dais. "I got the train times wrong and I started out by going to the wrong place."

"Glad you managed it at last, anyway," said Norman Prendergast. "This is young Henry Hollins, and that's his fossil."

"Hello," said Henry.

"Harrumph," muttered Professor Corrigan.

"And this is Mrs Murchison," said Norman Prendergast.

"Aaah-choo!" went Mrs Murchison.

"She can't stop sneezing," explained Norman Prendergast. "She's been like it for a fortnight."

At that moment, the studio manager got another message through his headphones, and he held up his hand. "One minute to go, everybody," he announced. "Quiet studio!"

74

There was an immediate silence. Henry Hollins watched the big second hand on a studio clock jerk round towards the sixty second mark. He had never known such a long minute in his life.

"Aaah-CHOO!" sneezed Mrs Murchison, louder than ever before, when forty-five seconds had gone by. The studio manager shot her a reproving glance and put a warning finger to his mouth. Ten more seconds ticked slowly away, and then—

Five—

Four—

Three—

Two—

One . . .

The programme was on the air.

"Good evening, everyone," said Norman Prendergast, flashing his broadest smile at Camera One. "Welcome to the *Half-Past-Six Show!*"

Henry watched, out of the corner of his eye, as Camera Two crept silently in towards his chair.

"Well, we have some very interesting people in the studio this evening," continued Norman Prendergast. "There's Mrs Arabella Murchison, from Doncaster, who has been sneezing continuously for two weeks, and doesn't know how to stop. And we have young Henry Hollins, from Staplewood, who found a dinosaur fossil last weekend, at Gunnersby Cove, while spending a day on the beach. Also, we've got with us a very old friend of the *Half-Past-Six Show!*,

Professor Horace Corrigan, who has come along to tell us what *he* thinks of Henry's fossil. But, first of all this evening, we're going to talk to—or rather *listen* to—Mrs Arabella Murchison."

Norman Prendergast turned to Mrs Murchison, smiled, and waited politely for her to sneeze. Mrs Murchison's nose trembled, her head twitched. Camera Three was pointing at Mrs Murchison, waiting for her to sneeze. Up in the control box, Julian Derwent-Smith, his assistant, and Albert Hollins, all watched the TV monitor screens, and waited for Mrs Murchison to sneeze. Ten million people all over the country were staring hard at Mrs Murchison on their television sets, waiting for her to sneeze. Mrs Murchison's nose twitched and her head trembled.

But nothing happened.

There was a long pause, and then Mrs Murchison glanced across at Norman Prendergast, looking rather sorry for herself.

"I can't do it," she said. "It's gone."

"Gone?" said Norman Prendergast.

"My sneezing," said Mrs Murchison. "It must have been all the excitement of being on the telly. I'm cured."

Norman Prendergast's mouth dropped open. "Surely you can manage one little 'atishoo' for the viewers?" he said.

But Mrs Murchison shook her head, firmly. "I'm

very sorry," she said, "but it's gone completely."

Norman Prendergast gave Mrs Murchison an icy smile. "Well," he said, "I'm sure all the viewers join me in wishing you well, and hoping that your sneezing doesn't return."

"Thank you very much, Norman," said Mrs Murchison, in a rather small voice.

Norman Prendergast turned away from Mrs Murchison, dismissing the poor lady, and he looked directly at Camera One. "And now for our second guest tonight. He's a young man who has made rather an exciting find . . ."

Henry Hollins could sense, rather than see, the probing eye of Camera Two moving even closer in on him, and also on the shiny fossil in his lap. He was aware too, of Camera Three, moving away from poor Mrs Murchison, who had let down not only the BBC but also the viewing public, by failing to manage a sneeze. Camera Three was crossing over towards Professor Corrigan.

Mrs Emily Hollins, snug in her armchair in Woodview, Nicholas Nickleby Close, Staplewood, leant forward and unwrapped a chocolate éclair as her son's head and shoulders filled the television screen in the corner of the living-room. And although she "tut-tutted" under her breath and said to herself, "I knew he'd forget to comb his hair", she really felt proud of her only boy. She was so overcome with emotion, in fact, that she popped the wrapping-paper instead of the éclair into her mouth and chewed on it for several seconds before realizing her mistake.

On the screen, the voice of Norman Prendergast addressed Henry. ". . . Henry Hollins, perhaps you'd like to tell the viewers yourself how you came across your fossil?"

Henry Hollins took a deep breath and then, suddenly, all of his nervousness was gone as he launched himself into his story. "Well," he said, "it was last Sunday afternoon when I found it, while I was at the seaside with my mum and dad . . ."

Up in the control box, Albert Hollins flushed up with importance as he heard himself mentioned on television. He leant forward in his chair.

"Cut to Camera One," said Julian Derwent-Smith, and the picture on the control box monitor screen changed to a close-up of the dinosaur fossil in Henry's lap.

"Go on, Henry," said the off-screen voice of Norman Prendergast.

As the camera stayed on the browny-green egg, Henry continued with his story. ". . . It was when I'd lost my kite up this cliff—I climbed up the cliff to get it back, and a piece of rock broke off, and I looked down and there it was—this dinosaur's egg fossil."

"Which all the viewers are looking at right at this moment," said Norman Prendergast. "Absolutely fascinating, Henry! And now perhaps you'll tell us how you knew it was a dinosaur's egg?"

In the studio, Henry Hollins thought for a moment and shook his head, slightly puzzled, before he answered. "I don't know," he said. "I mean, I've always been interested in dinosaurs—and I've got some other fossils at home—and I've read lots of books on the subject—but the books don't say much about dinosaurs' eggs." And he paused again and frowned, and then went on, "No, I don't know *how* I knew it was a dinosaur's egg. I just *knew*, that's all. As soon as I saw it, I *knew* what it was."

"Absolutely fascinating, Henry," said Norman Prendergast again. The television interviewer turned to the professor who was sitting on his other side. "Well, Professor Corrigan," he said. "I know that you were late arriving in the studio, and that you haven't had time to study Henry's fossil yet—but looking at it from where you're sitting now, perhaps you'd be kind enough to give us your opinion? What kind of dinosaur's egg do you think it is?"

Professor Horace Corrigan gave a lofty little smile, wriggled in his chair, and pushed all of his fingers through his spiky hair before he spoke. "Well, Norman," said the professor, giving a little chuckle, "from where I'm sitting, I can't say very much about the curious object in our young friend's lap, but I can say this much: whatever it is, it certainly isn't a dinosaur's egg—fossilized or otherwise."

"Isn't it?" said Norman Prendergast.

"No," said Professor Corrigan.

"Oh," said Norman Prendergast, rather flatly.

"Not in a million years," said Professor Corrigan, and added: "or two hundred million years, if it comes to that."

"Oh," said Norman Prendergast again.

"And it isn't any other kind of fossil either," went on the professor.

"What makes you say that?" asked Norman Prendergast.

The professor smiled his supercilious, professorial smile again. "Because it doesn't *look* like one, it's as simple as that. And I know that it isn't a dinosaur's fossilized egg—because alas, there is not one single dinosaur's egg of that shape or size in existence; not in any college, museum, or university in the world. And if such eggs do not exist, then it is not possible for this young man to be in possession of one, is it?"

"No," said Norman Prendergast, unhappily, "I take your point, Professor." The programme was not going at all the way that he wanted. First there had been the unfortunate business over Mrs Murchison being unable to raise so much as a sniff, let alone a sneeze, and now this let-down. The dinosaur fossil was turning out to be a damp squib. The programme had only been on the air for three minutes, and already both of his subjects for discussion had run up against brick walls. If he couldn't think of something, and fast, Norman Prendergast realized that the *Half-Past-Six Show!* that evening would consist mostly of total silence. The TV interviewer racked his brains, desperately. "Well, Professor," he said, in the faint hope of sparking off a discussion, "if it isn't a dinosaur fossil, what is it, in your opinion?"

Professor Corrigan shrugged, and spread wide his arms. "Who knows?" he said. "Something fashioned out of plastic, perhaps. I don't wish to disappoint our young friend, Henry, but it is possible that he has been the victim of a hoax." Professor Corrigan paused, and gazed at Henry for several seconds before he went on: "Or perhaps, even, he is trying to play a practical joke on us?"

"I'm not!" cried Henry, unable to contain himself. "And it isn't made of plastic, anybody can see that! It is a dinosaur's egg! I just know it is! And how can you say it doesn't look like one, if you've never seen one!"

Professor Corrigan smiled again and, once again, he shook his head, slowly and firmly.

Henry fell silent, his mouth shut tight. He had become aware of the fact that both Camera Two and Camera Three were now pointing straight at him, waiting for him to lose his temper again in front of ten million members of the viewing public.

Silence reigned supreme on the *Half-Past-Six Show!*

"Well . . ." said Norman Prendergast, uncomfortably, as he looked at Henry, and then turned his gaze on Professor Corrigan, and "Well . . ." he said again. "Haven't you got anything to add to your previous statement, Professor?"

"What else is there to say?" said the professor, "It's obviously a fake."

More silence, broken this time by the urgent ringing of the yellow telephone that was fixed next to Norman Prendergast's chair and which provided a direct line to the control box. The television interviewer snatched it up. "Yes?" he said.

"This is an absolute disaster!" It was the voice of Julian Derwent-Smith that thundered at the other end of the line.

"I know," mumbled Norman Prendergast, miserably.

"Look here," said Julian Derwent-Smith, "I've got some old film up here of some Morris Dancers, we're going to put that on now to pass the time. Introduce it now, would you—if you think you can manage it without making a total hash of things!"

"Righty-ho," said Norman Prendergast, and putting down the telephone he managed a weak smile for the benefit of the watching cameras. "Well!" he began. "That seems to conclude the subject of dinosaur fossils for this evening. And now we're going to move on to an *extra* item we have for you. Morris Dancing. Which is *always* topical. *Especially* at this time of year. And we're going to treat you now to some excellent film of some typically topical Morris Men—dancing."

"Cut to film!" said Julian Derwent-Smith in the control box.

Six jolly men wearing straw hats, and with handkerchiefs tied at their elbows and knees, danced into a village square on the television monitor screens.

Julian Derwent-Smith flung his head into his hands. "Disastervillle," he moaned. "Total disasterville."

Albert Hollins, sitting beside Mr Derwent-Smith, gave an embarrassed cough and said nothing.

The sleek, black BBC limousine was at a standstill. Albert Hollins poked his head out of the open window, for the third time in three minutes, and surveyed the long line of motionless traffic that stretched along the bypass road. Then, ducking his head back into the car, he pressed the communicating window button.

"It goes on for miles," he observed, gloomily, to the uniformed chauffeur. "Miles and miles—we'll be stuck here all night at this rate."

"It was you that wanted to try the bypass, sir," said the chauffeur. "Personally speaking, I much prefer the dual carriageway."

"That was coming *off* the motorway, I meant," said Albert. "Going back to Staplewood is a different kettle of fish entirely. It works the other way round then—it's the bypass that's always jam-packed and the dual carriageway is clear."

"That's as may be, sir," said the BBC chauffeur, "but it's a bit late to tell me now."

Albert Hollins slumped back, sulkily, in his seat. By his estimation, they wouldn't get back to Staplewood before nightfall. He wished that he had never agreed to go to the studios in the first place. It had been an entire waste of an evening. Not only that, but his son had succeeded in making a complete fool of himself on TV. And to think, thought Albert, that he had told several of his friends at the factory to watch the *Half-Past-Six Show!* that evening. And he felt a cold chill pass through his body as he suddenly remembered that he had told no less a personage than the head of the Garden Gnomes Department, Mr Cecil Grimsdyke Jnr himself, to watch it too. What must Mr Grimsdyke be thinking of the Hollins family now? It was all Henry's fault, of course. But then, wasn't that usually the case? Whenever anything went wrong for the Hollinses, young Henry was always at the back of things—somewhere. Another thought occurred to Albert, and he turned and fixed his son with a questioning stare.

"It wasn't true, was it?" he demanded. "What that professor chap said? It wasn't some sort of practical joke—that thingy?" Albert nodded at the dinosaur fossil that lay in Henry's lap.

"No!" said Henry, stoutly. "You know it isn't—you were there when I found it at Gunnersby Cove."

"I was there when you *said* you found it," said

Albert. "But where it came from, I don't know, I wouldn't put anything past you, not after tonight. You've not only made a fool of yourself, you know, you've made a fool of me as well. I don't know how I'm going to look anybody in the face at the factory tomorrow. And what am I going to say to Mr Grimsdyke in the morning, when I take him in his cup of coffee and his ginger biscuits? And what's Mr Grimsdyke going to say to *me?* That's more to the point." Albert Hollins lapsed into silence, and contemplated his miserable future.

Henry Hollins was also silent. He sat clutching tight to his fossil. It *was* a dinosaur's egg. He knew it was. He didn't care what the professor had said. He was the proud possessor of a genuine fossilized dinosaur's egg—the only one of its kind in the world.

Albert Hollins gave his son a sour look, sniffed, and spoke again. "I know this much," he said, "that thingy's going back where it belongs, when we get home—in the dustbin. And this time it isn't coming out."

Henry Hollins clutched his dinosaur fossil tighter than ever.

# 6

Standing by the garden gate with his school satchel slung round his neck, Henry Hollins watched as his father backed the family car out of the garage and into Nicholas Nickleby Close.

"Good morning, Dad!" Henry yelled across to Albert like a dutiful son, giving him an angelic smile, as he went on: "Have a good day at the office! Drive carefully—no speeding!"

Albert Hollins paused before driving off, and cast his son a suspicious glance. It was not like Henry, Albert mused to himself, to show such interest in his well-being. "Fat lot of chance I shall get to speed anywhere," he called back, "the traffic will be nose-to-tail all the way to the factory, once I get out on to Micawber Avenue."

With which, Albert Hollins put his foot down hard on the accelerator and sped off, with both sound and smoke roaring from the car's exhaust.

Henry Hollins stood waving to his father from the garden gate until Albert's car had turned the corner and was out of sight. Then Henry turned and ran back along the garden path and round the side of the house. Hastily, he tugged off the lid from the dustbin and lifted out the dinosaur fossil from its resting-place on top of a discarded old woollen cardigan. After a moment's thought, he lifted out the cardigan too and wrapped it carefully around the fossil.

Going into the house through the back door, he tiptoed across the kitchen and into the hall. He could hear the steady hum of the vacuum cleaner coming from the living-room as he made his way, stealthily, up the bedroom stairs. Then, just as he reached the bend in the stairs, and was complimenting himself on his good luck, he heard the vacuum cleaner being switched off, and his mother's voice calling out to him:

"Henry—is that you?"

"Yes, Mum."

"I thought you'd left for school five minutes ago?"

"I did, Mum, but I forgot something—my Geography book—it's in my bedroom. I had to come back for it."

"Hurry up then. You're going to be late unless you look sharp!"

Thankfully, during all this conversation, his mother did not once pop her head round the living-room door, and so she did not discover that he had rescued the dinosaur fossil from out of the rubbish yet again. When Henry heard his mother switch on the vacuum cleaner once more, he raced up the remaining stairs and on to the landing. Henry hesitated and wondered where the best place would be to hide the dinosaur's egg? Not in his own bedroom, he decided, for it was his mother's habit to go through his bedroom like a tornado, from top to bottom, once a week, with the particular object of hunting out any new treasures that Henry might store there. The spare bedroom, he knew, would have been the ideal place to hide the fossil, but that room was scheduled to be refurnished and redecorated shortly, and at the moment it didn't contain a stick of furniture.

For one daring and breathtaking moment, Henry even considered hiding the fossil inside his parents' bedroom, on top of the wardrobe, but he reluctantly dismissed the thought, marvelling at his own courage for even contemplating the idea.

So where then, he wondered? And it was at that moment that his glance fell on the airing-cupboard. Of *course*, he thought, the very place! For he knew that although his mother was in and out of the airing-cupboard several times a day in search of fresh linen, she never looked down behind the hot-water tank. Once, when Henry had been about five years old, he now remembered, he had hidden a teddy bear behind the hot-water tank and promptly forgotten about it. The teddy bear had remained there for several months, unnoticed, until by chance, he had rediscovered it himself.

And having taken the decision, Henry moved quickly. He opened the airing-cupboard door, knelt down, laid the woollen cardigan down on the floor behind the water tank, and gently nestled the fossil on top of the cardigan. He then rose to his feet and, after satisfying himself that the fossil was well and truly out of sight, shut the airing-cupboard door, ran down the stairs, out of the house, and set off for school.

"Hollins! I'm speaking to you, lad! Did you hear what I said? *Hollins!*"

With difficulty, Henry dragged himself out of his daydream world of prehistoric forests populated with giant dinosaurs, back into his real-life existence and the humdrum English lesson.

"Me, sir?" he said.

"Yes, you, sir!" snapped Mr Popplewell, Henry's English teacher. Nigel Popplewell was tall and thin with a beaky nose and he towered menacingly over Henry's desk. "Now that you're safely back in the land of the living," he went on, "perhaps you'd be kind enough to tell me what I've been talking about while you've been dozing in the back row?"

"Er . . ." Henry thought hard. "Was it about Oliver Twist, sir? Asking for more?"

"You know what you're asking for, Hollins, don't you?" growled Mr Popplewell. "A thick ear. And you're going to get one too, if you don't buck your ideas up, smartly, lad! No, it was not Oliver Twist. For your information, Hollins, the rest of the class and myself have been turning our attentions to Barnaby Rudge for the past ten minutes. Mind you, I don't suppose we can expect you to take much part in English lessons, can we? Not now you've become a

TV star?" Mr Popplewell's reference to Henry's television appearance caused an appreciative giggle to run around the form-room. The English teacher continued: "Hands up all those boys who watched our famous young colleague on the goggle-box last night."

Out of the corner of his eye, Henry saw about eight or nine of his classmates shoot their hands up in the air.

"Is that *all* ?" Mr Popplewell went on. "Then for the benefit of the not-so-fortunate majority, allow me to inform you that our own inimitable associate, Mr Henry Hollins, appeared on television yesterday evening in the role of natural historian and palaeontologist . . ." Mr Popplewell paused, and looked around the class. "Hands up all those who can tell me what a palaeontologist does!"

The eight or nine hands that were already raised went down, slowly, and no more rose to take their place.

Mr Popplewell shook his head, disapprovingly. "Nobody?" he said. "What about you, Hollins? Surely you know what a palaeontologist is?"

"Yes, sir," said Henry.

"Then don't hide your light under a bushel, lad," said Mr Popplewell. "Get up on your feet." Henry rose. "Now," said Mr Popplewell, "kindly inform these ignoramuses what a palaeontologist does."

"He's a man who studies fossils, sir."

"Exactly, Hollins! And you consider yourself to be a bit of a palaeontologist, don't you?"

"No, sir."

"'No, sir'? What do you mean, Hollins, 'No, sir'? If you *don't* consider yourself to be a bit of a palaeontologist, perhaps you'd be good enough to tell me, and the rest of your form, what you were doing on the *Half-Past-Six Show!* last night?"

Henry blinked, nervously, and looked around the room at the grinning faces that were all turned towards him enjoying his embarrassment. "Well, sir . . ." he began, and then paused and licked his lips.

"Come along, Hollins," said Mr Popplewell. "We're waiting. We're all hanging on your every word. Right, boys?"

"Right, sir!" yelled a chorus of voices.

"Well, sir," said Henry again, "I went to the seaside last Sunday and I got stuck up this cliff and I found this fossil."

"Did you?"

"Yes, sir. It's a big fossilized dinosaur's egg. It was in the rock half-way up the cliff, sir."

"Now, that's not quite true, Hollins, is it?"

"Yes, sir, it is, sir," said Henry Hollins stoutly. "I brought it back to Staplewood and first there was a bit in the *Guardian* about it, and then I was asked to go on the telly and be interviewed, sir."

Mr Popplewell shook his head again, slowly, and then he turned and spoke to the rest of the class.

"Hands up, again," he said, "all of those boys who watched the *Half-Past-Six Show!* last night."

The same eight or nine hands as before shot into the air and waved about, excitedly. "Please, sir, me, sir!"

"I did, sir!"

"Me too, sir!" shouted various voices.

"Right then," said Mr Popplewell, pointing at one of the boys whose hand was raised. "You, Stigwood, up on your feet, lad!"

Rory Stigwood, a ginger-headed boy with a tie that was always crooked, rose in his desk. "Yes, sir?" he said.

"Now, Stigwood, I want you to give us your version of what happened on the *Half-Past-Six Show!* last night."

Stigwood wrinkled up his nose like a rabbit sniffing a carrot, scratched his head, and thought. "Well, sir," he said at last, "there was this woman on the telly who was supposed to sneeze all the time, sir, only when it came to it, she didn't sneeze at all."

"I don't mean that part of the programme, Stigwood, I want to know what happened when Hollins came on?"

"I don't know, sir. I went into the kitchen to have my tea then."

"Sit down, Stigwood, you hopeless oaf."

Stigwood took his seat to cries of "Good old

93

Stiggy!" and "Trust you, Stiggy!" and "Stigwood strikes again!"

"You, Denison," said Mr Popplewell, pointing at another boy who had his hand in the air.

"Yes, sir?"

"Did you observe friend Hollins on the idiot box last night?"

"Yes, sir."

"Up on your feet then, Denison, and enlighten your form-mates as to what it was that Hollins was up to on the small screen."

"Yes, sir," said Denison, a studious-looking boy with glasses and freckles on his nose. "Well, sir, there was Henry and this professor on the telly, sir, and Henry had this big piece of stone . . ."

"It *wasn't* a piece of stone," interrupted Henry, "it was a fossil!"

"Silence, Hollins!" said Mr Popplewell. "Let Denison have his say. Continue, Denison."

"Well, sir," said Denison, "it *was* a piece of stone, sir, or plastic or something—anyway, it definitely wasn't a fossil, because this professor said so."

"Can you remember the name of the professor, Denison?"

"Er . . . Wasn't it Professor Corrigan, sir?"

"It was, Denison. Professor Horace Corrigan, in fact. And one of the foremost palaeontologists of our time, I suppose even you would agree with that, Hollins?"

"He is quite well known," admitted Henry.

"Thank you, Hollins," said Mr Popplewell. "And now, Denison, would you tell the form what the professor had to say about Hollins' fossil?"

"He said it wasn't a fossil, sir," said Denison. "He said it was a fake, sir."

"He's wrong!" blurted Henry. "It *is* a fossil!"

"I said, 'silence', Hollins!" said Mr Popplewell. "You might attempt to argue with your elders and betters on television—but don't try it on in *my* classroom."

"But it's *true,* sir," insisted Henry. "It really is a dinosaur fossil."

"Rubbish, lad," replied Mr Popplewell. "Are you trying to tell me that you are more informed about fossils than the famous and eminent Professor Horace Corrigan?"

"No, sir."

"Well, then?"

"Only professors aren't always right, are they, sir? I mean, it wouldn't be the first time that a scientist had made a mistake about prehistoric times."

"Explain yourself, Hollins?"

"Well, sir," said Henry, "there was the case of the coelacanth, wasn't there?"

Mr Popplewell looked around the room at the blank faces that were staring back at him. "Just a minute, Hollins," he said. "Hands up any boy who has any idea what a coelacanth is," he said. Not a hand was raised in the whole classroom. "Come out here to the front, Hollins," said Mr Popplewell. Henry rose from his desk and walked out to join his teacher at the front of the class. "Now," said Mr Popplewell, "tell us about the coelacanth."

"Well, sir . . ." began Henry.

"Not me," said Mr Popplewell, waving an arm at the form-room full of boys. "Explain it to this ignorant lot out there."

"Well," Henry began again, "there was this fish called the coelacanth, and it lived about three hundred and fifty million years ago. And everybody thought it was extinct, like all the other prehistoric fishes."

"And did they have a reason to think that, Hollins?" said Mr Popplewell.

"Yes, sir," said Henry. "There weren't any fossils to prove otherwise, sir. Nobody had ever found any coelacanth fossils that were less than sixty million years old—so they believed that the coelacanth must have become extinct about sixty million years ago."

Mr Popplewell nodded again "I see," he said. "Go on."

"And then somebody caught a coelacanth alive, in 1938. And another was caught in 1952. And the people that caught the coelacanth were just ordinary fishermen—but they proved that scientists aren't always right, didn't they, sir?"

"They did, Hollins," said Mr Popplewell. "They

did indeed. And you intend to do the same with this . . . this *thing* that you've found, do you?"

"I'd like to, sir."

"I see. Good luck to you, Hollins. Sit down, boy."

Henry went back to his desk and, as he took his seat, the bell rang in the hall, signifying the end of the lesson. Mr Popplewell glanced at his watch, in some surprise. "You've succeeded in one thing, Hollins," he said. "You've managed to turn my English class into a Natural History lesson. All right! All right, a bit less noise the rest of you! Stigwood, stop banging those books about, lad!"

One by one, the boys got their things together for the next class and they began to form into a line by the door. Mr Popplewell crossed down between the rows of desks to where Henry Hollins was collecting his own books together, a little slower than the other boys.

"There's only one thing that bothers me, Hollins," said Mr Popplewell, "if you are right about this dinosaur egg of yours."

"I *am* right, sir," said Henry.

"*If* you are," said Mr Popplewell, with a smile, "it isn't going to turn out to be not extinct—like the coelacanth, is it? I mean, you aren't expecting to wake up one morning and find that it's hatched into a dinosaur, are you?"

"I don't think so, sir," said Henry, also with a smile.

"Good, I'm relieved to hear it," said Mr Popplewell. "Off you go."

That night, Emily Hollins sat up in bed with a start and nudged her sleeping husband, sharply, in the ribs. "Albert!" she hissed.

Albert Hollins grunted and rolled over on to his other side.

"Albert!" hissed Emily again, giving him an even sharper jab in his side.

"Ow!" groaned Albert, as he woke up, "That hurt!"

"Ssshhh!" said Emily. "I think we've got a burglar—I heard a noise."

"You're always hearing noises," muttered Albert, "every night of the week."

"But this was a different *kind* of noise," whispered Emily, anxiously.

"It's *always* a different kind of noise, every night, according to you," grumbled Albert. "What kind of a noise was it this time? Did it sound like the front door being broken into, or the sitting-room window sliding up, or was it the sound of menacing footsteps in the downstairs hall; your noises usually fit into the general category of one of those."

"Not tonight, Albert," said Emily. "It was a sort of, well, a *cracking* noise."

"A cracking noise?"

98

"Mmmm. And it sounded close—as if it was on the upstairs landing."

"Go back to sleep."

"I shan't be able to sleep, Albert, not until you've been to the bedroom door and had a look."

With a long-suffering sigh, Albert Hollins got out of bed and tiptoed across the bedroom floor. "Ow!" he cried, as he groped in the darkness for the bedroom door and found it with his right big toe. Still muttering to himself, he opened the door and glanced both ways along the moonlit landing. "Is there anybody there?" he called. But there was no reply, and the house was still and silent.

"What did I tell you?" he said to Emily, as he closed the bedroom door again. Then, "Ouch!" he cried, as he floundered in the darkness for the end of the bed, and discovered it with his left big toe. A moment later he gave a third cry of pain, "Oooh!" he groaned as he fell over the wooden box which contained the three thousand and five hundred soup-tin labels that Emily was collecting on behalf of the Dublin pandas.

"Are you all right, Albert?" asked Emily, as her husband clambered back into bed, still groaning to himself.

"Go back to sleep," said Albert.

"Yes, dear," said Emily. "But I *did* hear something—a sort of cracking noise. You don't think you ought to go downstairs and have a look, do you?"

No reply.

"Albert?"

"ZZZZzzzz," snored Albert, already fast asleep again.

"That reminds me of something," murmured Emily to herself. "I must get down to selling those raffle tickets for the new anaesthetic equipment at the Little Dorrit Hospital . . ." With which, she too fell fast asleep.

# 7

"Do you want to know what I think?" asked Emily Hollins, passing her husband the salad cream. Receiving no reply from either her husband or her son, Emily proceeded to tell them anyway: "I think we've got mice."

"Off she goes again," chuckled Albert, giving Henry a wink, and dolloping salad cream all over his sardine salad. "Last night we had burglars, according to your mother, and tonight we've got mice."

Henry smiled but said nothing, there were times he had decided, when it was best to stay neutral.

"Well, I did hear something last night. A sort of cracking noise, up on the bedroom landing—but perhaps it wasn't burglars after all . . ."

"Ah!" put in Mr Hollins.

". . . perhaps," continued Mrs Hollins, "I heard mice."

"Last night?"

"Mmmm."

"On the bedroom landing?"

"Mmmm."

"I very much doubt it."

"*Why* not?" said Emily.

"Well, for one thing," replied Albert, emphasizing

his point by waving a spring onion at his wife, "what were these mice of yours doing—cracking walnuts?" And Mr Hollins gave Henry another wink, and continued: "And why were they up on the bedroom landing? Mice, as I understand them, are inclined to limit their activities to the lower parts of buildings: kitchens and dining-rooms and so forth, where there's grub to be had. What say you, Henry?"

"Don't know, Dad," said Henry, preserving his neutrality.

"There are some things *you* don't know, then," observed Emily to her husband. "Because we *have* got mice—most definitely—and they *are* up on the landing, and I'll prove it." And, as she spoke, Emily Hollins drew something from her apron pocket and held it up for Albert and Henry to see.

The object that Emily was displaying was one of Albert's socks. At least, it *had* been one of Albert's socks—for now it was a sock no longer: the foot was missing.

"What's happened to that?" gasped Albert.

"The mice have chewed it," said Emily.

"Well, I'll be blessed," said Albert, "I've never heard of mice chewing socks before! Are you sure it wasn't a moth?"

"Moths make holes—not chew whole feet off things," said Emily. "Besides, you'd need a moth as big as a golden eagle to do that much damage to a sock."

"True," admitted Albert. "Where did you find it?"

"That's what I'm telling you," Emily went on. "It was upstairs—in the airing-cupboard."

And it was only at the mention of the airing-cupboard that Henry sat up and began to take note of his parents' conversation.

"I don't know about a big moth," observed Albert, judiciously, "but it must be a mighty big mouse by the look of that sock—either that or there must be a lot of them. Did you see any other signs of them?"

"What?" asked Emily.

"Why, mice!" said Albert. "Did you see any mouse-droppings or anything else in the airing-cupboard? Behind the hot-water tank, for instance. They might have made a nest behind there, where it's nice and warm and cosy."

"I didn't *look* behind the hot-water tank," said Emily. "I was leaving that to you. I can't bear the sight of mice, so I'm certainly not going to go out of my way to look for them."

Albert Hollins selected a deep-red radish from a saucer, popped it into his mouth and chewed on it for several seconds before he spoke. "All right," he said, "as soon as I've finished my dinner I'll go up there and have a good scout round." And he reached out and picked up a second radish that was a richer colour even than the one before.

"Excuse me," said Henry, pushing back his chair and rising from the table.

"Where do you think you're going?" said Albert, through a mouthful of radish.

"Upstairs."

"What for?"

"Er . . . to the bathroom," said Henry, using the first excuse that came into his head.

"I do wish you'd go before you sit down at the table," said his mother. "Go on then—hurry up—I've just poured your tea out."

Henry raced up the bedroom stairs two at a time. He had to get his dinosaur fossil out of the airing-cupboard and into another hiding-place before his father had his "good scout round". Up on the bedroom landing, Henry opened the door of the airing-cupboard and knelt down. He put his hand round the back of the hot-water tank and felt about on the woollen cardigan for the fossil.

Henry's face fell and he groaned with dismay. The fossil was no longer in one piece. In fact, it was in fragments. Henry withdrew his hand, bringing out a couple of small fossil pieces. The heat from the tank, he guessed, must have caused the fossil to break. He turned the pieces over in his hand, and was surprised to discover that the fossil egg had not been solid. What he was holding, were two pieces of shell.

Deciding to look for a larger piece, in order to examine it more closely, Henry stuck his arm behind the hot-water tank again, stretching as far as he could go. In the darkest, farthest corner behind the tank,

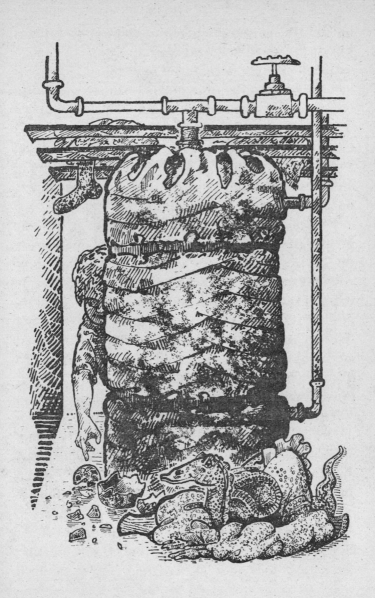

his hand encountered something. It was warm. It was soft. It was smooth. It was breathing.

Gently, and with infinite care, Henry tucked his hand and forearm underneath whatever-it-was and lifted out the living body.

Henry Hollins stared down at the thing that nestled cosily along his arm. He gulped once, and then twice, and then a third time. After that he stopped gulping and just sat there on his heels, gazing down, open-mouthed.

The thing—for he could not put a name to it—was greeny-grey in colour and measured about seventy centimetres from tip to tail. In shape, it was unlike anything he had ever seen before. It had a dumpy puppy-like body; a scrawny neck with a sort of lizardy head on the end; four pudgy stumps of legs; a long thin tail like an overgrown mouse. Out of the closed mouth of the reptile—if reptile it was—there trailed a strand of wool from Albert's sock. The creature was fast asleep.

It was impossible, but true nevertheless.

The dinosaur egg had not been fossilized after all. In some fantastic, inexplicable and miraculous way, the dinosaur's egg had hatched out in the heat of the airing-cupboard. What Henry Hollins was cradling in his arms was a baby dinosaur.

Henry, who was still kneeling on the floor, sitting back on his heels, hugged the warm, soft creature closer to himself, and stroked its wrinkled stomach

106

with one hand. At that moment, the creature opened one eye, sleepily, and fixed Henry with a solemn stare. Then, as Henry continued to stroke the creature's tummy, its eyelid slipped shut again, drowsily. It was fast asleep once more. Henry sat motionless, holding the baby dinosaur in his arms.

"Henry!" It was his mother's voice that called up from the foot of the bedroom stairs. "*Henry!* Can you hear me?"

"Yes, Mum!" Henry was aware of his own voice calling back to his mother.

"What are you *doing* up there all this time?"

"Nothing, Mum!" he replied, for he could hardly call down: "playing with a baby dinosaur".

"Come along then, dear!" shouted Emily. "I can't clear the table until you finish your dinner—and I've *so* many things to do. I wanted to search out some jumble today for the vicar's organ-pipes. *And* I faithfully promised I'd find something for the Church Fête tombola."

"Just coming, Mum," called Henry.

To his relief, Henry heard his mother going back into the dining-room, and then the sound of the door closing behind her. Thoughts raced through his head. He had to make up his mind, quickly, what he was going to do about the new-born dinosaur.

He could, of course, confront his parents and show them the prehistoric baby reptile. But what good would that do? They certainly wouldn't allow him to keep it as a pet, of that he was quite sure. His mother, he decided, would probably raffle it off in aid of the repairs to the church organ. As for his father, Albert Hollins had already refused his son the right to keep a dinosaur egg in the house, and so he most definitely would not allow a living dinosaur to stay under his roof for five minutes—particularly after the damage it had done to Albert's sock!

No, Henry decided, there was no point at all in telling his parents about the weird and wonderful happening that had taken place at Number 23 Nicholas Nickleby Close—certainly not at that moment. He knew that he would have to get the creature out of the house at once, and that meant that there was only one possible place for it: the garden shed.

Henry Hollins clambered to his feet, scooping up the baby dinosaur in his arms as he rose. "Come on," he muttered to the sleeping creature, "it's not as warm and cosy as the airing-cupboard, but it's going to have to do to be going on with."

Then, holding the baby dinosaur close to his chest, under his jacket, Henry tiptoed down the stairs, along the hall, and up to the front door. He opened the door quietly. Then he slipped out round the corner of the house as the door slammed shut behind him.

In the dining-room, Emily Hollins looked up with a puzzled frown. "Wasn't that the front door?" she said.

Albert Hollins swallowed down the last of the radishes and burped. "Pardon," he said.

"I said, 'wasn't that the front door that just slammed?'" repeated Emily.

"I know you did," said Albert. "I heard you. I said 'pardon' because the radishes made me burp."

Emily Hollins gave her husband a cross look, shook her head despairingly, and picked up Henry's plate on which was his half-eaten sardine salad. "If it *was* the front door," she said, "it must have been our Henry going out before he's finished his dinner." Emily crossed into the kitchen with Henry's unfinished meal, still complaining: "I can't imagine what's got into our Henry of late; you'll have to have a serious talk with him, Albert."

"Pardon?" said Mr Hollins, as his wife came flouncing out of the kitchen.

"I don't know!" said Emily, with a sigh. "You and those radishes! You'll have to stop eating so many if they make you burp all the time!"

"I didn't say 'pardon' that time *because* of the radishes," said Albert. "I said 'pardon' just then because I didn't hear what you said—you were in the kitchen. What *did* you say?"

Emily Hollins let out another exasperated sigh. "*I* don't know," she said, "I've forgotten." And she continued with her task of clearing the dinner things from the table.

"I know what I'm going to do," said Albert, pushing back his chair and getting to his feet. "I'm going upstairs to have that scout round in the

109

airing-cupboard. I'm going to see if I can find those sock-eating high-rise dwelling mice of yours." With which, he left the dining-room.

Henry Hollins, in the shed at the bottom of the garden, lowered the sleeping baby dinosaur carefully into the nest he had fashioned in the bottom of an old packing-case. He had lined the packing-case with straw and wood-shavings, making it warm and soft and comfortable. But the prehistoric creature did not seem to appreciate the trouble to which Henry had gone to make its home. The dinosaur wriggled and struggled and grunted and kicked its pudgy legs in the air, irritably. It was wide-awake.

"I expect it's because you're hungry," said Henry. "I shouldn't think that sock of Dad's was all that appetizing anyway." Then, giving the dinosaur a parting rub on its tummy—a gesture of affection that it seemed to enjoy—Henry went out of the garden shed and walked up the path towards the house.

Peering over the window-sill, cautiously, Henry saw that the kitchen was empty. He opened the kitchen door and went in. His half-eaten dinner, still on its plate, was on the kitchen table along with a pile of dirty crockery. Henry picked up the sardine salad and went out.

As the kitchen door closed on Henry, his father looked in from the hall, carrying a grubby woollen cardigan. "Is that you, Emily?" said Albert. "Are you in here?"

"I'm in the sitting-room!" Emily's voice called out to her husband.

Scratching his head, puzzled, Albert closed the door to the kitchen and went into the sitting-room. He found Emily watching the television, taking a well-earned breather before she tackled the washing-up.

"You were right, Emily," said Albert, holding up the woollen cardigan. "We have got mice in the airing-cupboard—they made their nest in my old cardigan."

"That's strange," said Emily. "I'm sure I put that cardigan into the dustbin yesterday—I meant to send it to the Noise Abatement Society, but I'd posted that parcel off the day before."

Albert frowned and scratched his head again. "Well, I never!" he said. "They must be whopping big mice all right! I've never heard of a mouse dragging a cardigan up a flight of bedroom stairs before!"

"What did I tell you before dinner about them eating a pair of socks?" said Emily, triumphantly.

Albert, giving up the problem of the giant-sized mice, turned his eyes to the television. "What are you watching?" he asked.

"It's the *Half-Past-Six Show!*" said Emily. "It's going to be an interesting programme. There's going to be a man on tonight who blows cigarette smoke out of his ears."

"Isn't there a cowboy film on the other side?" asked Albert, his interest perking up as he crossed and switched the TV set over to the opposite channel.

Emily, who was not mad about cowboy films, got to her feet. "I'll go and get on with the washing-up," she said.

Albert stretched himself out, comfortably, and settled down to watch the film.

Down at the bottom of the Hollins' garden, in the garden shed, Henry pushed another piece of lettuce into the creature's mouth. The baby dinosaur chomped on the lettuce with obvious satisfaction, using the tiny rows of pin-pointed, sharp teeth with which it had been born. The dinosaur swallowed down the lettuce and opened its jaws, hungrily, for more. Henry crammed another piece of lettuce into the waiting mouth. It had already turned down the offer of half a sardine.

"I don't know what kind of dinosaur you are," said Henry to his new-found friend, "but I do know this much: "you're not a meat-eater—you're one of the plant-eating kind."

The baby dinosaur grunted again, and chewed its lettuce, happily.

# 8

Albert Hollins folded his Sunday newspaper, neatly, and put it on the table. He crossed to the window and looked out. The sun was shining. Not so much as a breeze stirred in the branches of the trees beyond the garden. A bee droned, lazily, and hovered above a rosebush. A church bell rang out from somewhere in the centre of Staplewood. A thrush was peck-pecking unsuccessfully in search of worms on the Hollins' lawn. It was a perfect Sunday morning.

Mr Hollins looked up at the cloudless sky and rubbed his hands together, briskly. "Of course," he said, "what we could do is get the car out and drive as far as Peggotty's Point for the day."

"Could we, Dad?" said Henry, thinking to himself how much nicer it would be if he could only take his dinosaur along too.

"Mmmm," said Mr Hollins. "We could take a picnic."

"That *would* be lovely," said Mrs Hollins, who had just entered the room carrying a big wooden box.

"Mmmm," repeated Mr Hollins, and then continued: "Only it's such a beautiful day that it will be quite impossible to move on the roads for Sunday drivers."

"Does that mean that we can't go then?" asked Henry.

"Mmmm," said Mr Hollins, nodding his head, sagely.

"I suppose that's just as well really," said Emily. "I've got to sort all these out into different varieties." And so saying, she upended the wooden box so that three thousand five hundred and seventeen soup-tin labels cascaded to the floor.

Mr Hollins frowned and looked down, glumly, at the carpet that was thick with soup-tin labels. "I think I'll get the mower out and give that lawn a bit of a going-over this morning," he said.

"I'll do that for you, Dad," said Henry, quickly.

"Will you really?" said Albert, in some surprise.

"Well now," said Emily, squatting on the floor and starting out by making one pile for *Cream of Tomato* and another one for *Minestrone,* "what a helpful young man our Henry's turning into of late!"

Albert Hollins nodded. "All right, son," he said. "You tackle the lawn and I'll do some weeding down the vegetable patch."

"I did the weeding yesterday, Dad," said Henry.

"Did you?" said Albert, more surprised than before.

Henry nodded.

"I thought you didn't like gardening?" said Albert.

"I didn't before—but I do now," said Henry. "In fact, I think I'll get the mower out and make a start on the lawn right this minute." And giving his mother a cheery, dutiful smile, Henry walked out of the room.

"My word," said Emily, starting new piles for *Thick Green Pea* and *Cock-a-Leekie*, "but he *has* changed for the better of late!"

Albert rubbed pensively at the back of his neck with his left hand. "I don't understand it," he said. "I just don't understand it, at all!"

Over a fortnight had passed since the hatching out of the dinosaur egg and, despite what Mrs Hollins had said, in those two weeks and few short days, Henry Hollins had not changed at all.

Henry Hollins hated gardening. He loathed weeding the vegetable patch and if there was one thing he loathed *more* than weeding the vegetable patch it was mowing the lawn. Henry had been forced to take on all of these unpleasant extra duties however, because of his dinosaur. Henry's dinosaur had greatly increased in size over the past two weeks. It was now over a metre long from tail-tip to horny jaw and, when it raised itself up on its stumpy hind legs, it could easily peer out of the window of the garden shed. In fact, the dinosaur had grown quite fond of raising itself up on its back legs and gazing out of the shed window, its long snout pressed up against the glass. Happily, as far as Henry was concerned, the window of the shed looked out over the back garden fence, and could not be seen from the house. Also, and even more happily, on the other side of the back-garden fence there was a spinney, and beyond the spinney lay fallow farmland. The dinosaur could, if it so desired, peer out of the window all day long without any chance of it being seen by anyone.

All the same, as Henry was fearfully well aware, it only required his father to push the lawn mower down as far as the bottom edge of the lawn—or his mother to stroll down to the vegetable patch in search of a cabbage or an apronful of peas—and for either parent to glance in at the garden-shed window at the same moment as the dinosaur chose to look out, and Henry's prehistoric pet would be a secret no longer.

There was another problem too, apart from the reptile's size. It was also beginning to make noises. Not loud noises, just playful grunts; but as the dinosaur grew bigger day by day, so too did the grunts grow louder. And although Henry had so far contrived to keep his parents away from the bottom of the garden, there was no way in which he could prevent the sounds of the dinosaur from travelling up the garden towards the rear of the house.

"Do you know what I think?" Emily had remarked only a couple of days before, when she had bustled into the kitchen from the garage with a sackful of milk-bottle tops to be counted.

"No," Albert had replied. "What do you think now, Emily?"

"I think that those people next door but one, at number twenty-five, have started keeping pigs."

"Pigs!" Albert had said, astonished.

And it had occurred to Henry, at the time, that his father would not have sounded more astonished if his mother had said "dinosaurs".

"That's right," Emily had replied. "Pigs—I've just heard them grunting."

"They can't keep pigs in Nicholas Nickleby Close," Albert had said. "We have to abide by *rules*; we're living on a council estate, not in a farmyard! No, you must be mistaken, Emily. They're probably rabbits."

"Rabbits don't grunt," Emily had observed, "pigs do."

"They smell too, do pigs," Albert had said, and then turning to his son, continued: "Nip outside, Henry, and take a deep sniff—if you can smell anything, we'll put in a complaint to the council."

And Henry had done as he had been told. He had gone outside and sniffed, deeply, then he had gone back into the house with a negative report. "I can't smell anything, Dad," Henry had said.

"There you are! What did I say!" Albert had cried, triumphantly. "If you can't sniff them, they can't be pigs. They *must* be rabbits."

"What about the grunts?" Emily had asked.

"P'raps they're guinea-pigs then," Albert had said. "They grunt, don't they?"

"No," Emily had argued. "Guinea-pigs squeal.

117

And they don't squeal so loudly that you can hear them two doors off."

But the subject had been dropped and, thankfully, Emily had not heard grunting again.

Even so, there was yet another problem that Henry had to contend with concerning the dinosaur. It was a problem that caused him more difficulty as day followed day. It was the problem of feeding the creature, for the dinosaur's appetite was, naturally, growing daily as the prehistoric reptile increased in size.

The dinosaur was now eating a bucketful of various greenstuffs every day. Its favourite food was, without a doubt, lawn cuttings. Whenever Henry mowed the lawn, the dinosaur watched him through a crack in the garden shed, its small, beady, bright eyes followed the progress of the mower, eagerly, as Henry pushed it up and down the lawn.

Second to lawn cuttings, and as part of its staple diet, the dinosaur had taken a fancy to clippings from the privet hedge. Now, as well as mowing the lawn, Henry was clipping the privet hedge regularly every few days. There were too, occasional *special* treats for the dinosaur from the vegetable patch, such as an odd lettuce or cabbage that was going to seed, or a handful of ferny carrot-tops.

But Henry knew full well that the dinosaur was growing beyond a diet of garden leftovers. There was a limit to the amount of cuttings you could get from a garden lawn that was not much bigger than a large-sized handkerchief; there was a limit to the number of times you could successfully trim a kitchen-garden privet hedge.

Besides, if the dinosaur continued to grow at its present rate, where was it all going to end?

*The* Diplodocus, *which roamed the earth in the Jurassic Period, 150 million years ago, measured as much as 29 metres in length and, because of its huge size and tiny mouth, spent most of its life eating.*

Henry snapped shut his dinosaur book, sighed and shook his head sadly as he stroked the hard bony hump on top of the reptile's head. "If you're going to grow up into a *Diplodocus*," said Henry to his monster pet, "a whole year's cuttings from our lawn wouldn't make you much more than a mid-morning snack."

The dinosaur nuzzled its leathery little head into Henry's stomach and playfully nipped at his fingers with thousands and thousands of tiny teeth. For the dinosaur's mouth, Henry had discovered, did not contain two rows of teeth like any creature of today, but held row upon row upon row of tiny pin-point teeth in both its upper and lower jaws.

"I don't think you *are* going to be a *Diplodocus* though," mused Henry, and then he chuckled to himself. "Whatever you turn into," he went on, "one of these fine days you're going to give that Professor Corrigan a shock!" Henry had not yet decided when he would announce the news of the dinosaur's existence to the world; he was biding his time for that. There were one or two people, he felt, who owed him an apology, and Professor Horace Corrigan was certainly one of them. Henry rubbed his clenched fist along the dinosaur's smooth, warm stomach and the leathery-skinned monster grunted with delight, rolled over on its back and rubbed its spine along the wooden floor of the garden shed. "Come on," said Henry, suddenly rising to his feet. "It's time for walkies."

Every evening, as the sun crept low into the early darkening sky, Henry Hollins took his dinosaur out into the garden for half an hour's exercise. It was quite safe for him to do this. Neither his mother nor his father ever strayed far from the television set after the evening's washing-up had been done.

As for the Hollins' neighbours in Nicholas Nickleby Close: on the right-hand side lived Edwin and Olive Prendergast, a young couple who were even greater telly addicts than Albert and Emily Hollins; and on the left-hand side there lived Norman Glissworthy, a middle-aged bachelor who spent his every evening playing darts in the local pub, the Edwin Drood Inn.

Both Henry Hollins and his dinosaur equally enjoyed their evening romps on the garden lawn. Henry had been trying, for several days now, to teach the dinosaur to bring back things, but without much success.

He tried again. "Fetch it, boy! Fetch! Fetch!

There's a good monster!" Henry yelled, hurling a stick across the garden for the umpteenth time that week. But tonight, the lumbering creature paid even less attention than usual to Henry's shouts and calls. The dinosaur chose instead to amble down to the bottom of the garden where it hung its head over the wooden railings and gazed across, rather mournfully, at the spinney on the other side of the fence.

Henry strolled down and joined the dinosaur, slipping his arm round its neck. Following the dinosaur's hungry gaze, he looked across at the dark, inviting spinney, and at the lush, green foliage on the trees and bushes. He could guess the creature's thoughts.

"All right, boy," said Henry, comforting the dinosaur. "I know there's lots to eat across there, and I *will* take you over." The dinosaur snuffled eagerly and rubbed its chest along the garden fence, very nearly pushing it down, as though it understood every word that Henry had said. "But we can't go tonight," the boy continued, "I'll take you over tomorrow though—after I've bought you a collar and lead."

Henry tugged at the dinosaur's neck, pulling it back towards the garden shed. The prehistoric creature gave in at last, and allowed itself to be dragged away from the fence; for although it was only a little over two weeks old, it was very strong and quite a handful to control. Then, as it allowed Henry

to lead it back to the shed, the dinosaur raised its head up at the evening sky, opened its mouth, and gave out a long, low-pitched soulful howl.

Emily Hollins, perched on the sofa in the sitting-room, leant forward and turned the volume control knob on the television set right down. "There! What did I say!" she exclaimed. "Didn't you hear that?"

"What?" asked Albert crossly. On the screen, he could see that the posse of goodie cowboys had managed to corner the gang of baddie cowboys in a one-way canyon, and that the final showdown was just about to commence. Albert was furious. A gunfight isn't a gunfight, he thought, without the sound of gunshot. "I can't hear anything at all", he muttered at Emily, "if you turn the sound off altogether!"

"I didn't mean did you hear anything on the telly," said Emily. "I meant did you hear that howl from those pigs next door but one?"

"No," said Albert, grumpily. "I didn't hear anything. Besides—pigs don't howl, they grunt." With which observation, Albert leant forward and turned up the volume control knob on the TV set.

The sound of ricocheting rifle-fire and the ker-spinging of revolver-shot echoed around and around the sitting-room at Number 23, Nicholas Nickleby Close.

It was an exciting battle that took place in the one-way canyon; a lot of the baddies and even some of the goodies bit the dust. It kept Albert Hollins on the edge of his seat, biting his nails, until the very end when, as usual, the goodies won.

# 9

The man in the pet shop held up yet another dog-collar for Henry's inspection. "This is the biggest one in the shop," he said.

"Yes," said Henry, "that should just about fit."

"Crikey-Moses!" said the man, as he wrapped up the collar along with a dog-lead that Henry had already chosen. "It must be a big 'un you've got! Alsatian, is it?"

"Er . . . no," said Henry, slightly flustered.

"I'll bet it's a St Bernard then?" said the man.

"That's right," said Henry, telling a lie in order to save himself from further awkward questions. He paid the man for the collar and lead and left the shop.

Henry Hollins had one more call to make before he went home.

The rather stout lady behind the counter in the public library, whose name was Miss Pamela Purvis, was turning over the pages of a thick book called *The History of Costume Through the Ages*. The town of Staplewood was holding its Annual Festival, called Dickens Week, in a few weeks' time, and Miss Pamela Purvis had been chosen to appear as Mrs Micawber in the Grand Procession that was going to take place through the High Street on the Saturday afternoon. Miss Purvis, who was designing her own Mrs Micawber costume, had just found the chapter headed *Victorian Fashions*, when Henry Hollins walked into the library and up to the counter.

"Excuse me," said Henry.

Pamela Purvis pushed *The History of Costume Through the Ages* to one side, regretfully, and blinked at Henry through her gold-rimmed spectacles. "Yes, young man," she said, "can I help you?"

"I ordered a book in here a couple of weeks ago," said Henry. "I wondered if you'd got it in yet?"

"What was the title?"

"*An Illustrated Encyclopedia of Dinosaurs*," said Henry.

"Just a minute," said Miss Purvis, and she turned away and began to flick through a card-index file.

Henry glanced around the book-lined walls of the library and suddenly found himself looking into the eyes of the uniformed attendant who was glowering back at him. It was the very same attendant, in fact, who had ordered Henry and his dinosaur fossil out of the library premises a few short weeks before.

Henry pretended not to recognize the attendant, and turned away to look at a poster on the wall. But the library official had recognized Henry, and was already striding across the polished floor towards him.

"Hey—you!" snapped the attendant, pulling up short beside Henry.

"Me?" said Henry, innocently.

"Yes, you. Aren't you the lad who came in here with a great big lump of rock?"

"No," replied Henry, truthfully.

"Oh, yes, you are!"

"No, I'm not. But I did come in once with a dinosaur fossil."

"And don't be cheeky," said the bad-tempered attendant. "Never mind what it was—you brought it in here, so don't try to deny it. What's that you've got under your arm now?"

Henry held up his brown-paper parcel. "Do you mean this?" he said. "It's just a dog-lead and a collar."

"Dog-leads, and collars, dinosaur fossils, lumps of rock!" grumbled the library attendant. "This is the Staplewood Public Library, you know—not a village jumble sale. Next thing we know, you'll be strolling in here with a full-size dinosaur!"

"I will, too, if you're not careful," thought Henry; but being a sensible lad he kept his thoughts to himself.

It was at that moment that Miss Purvis turned back from her card-index. "I'm afraid the book you wanted is still on loan," she said to Henry. "It's been borrowed by a Professor Horace Corrigan."

"Oh," said Henry out loud—and he added to himself: "I might have guessed it was him!"

"He's had it out for over two months," said Miss

Purvis. "I'll send him one of our cards telling him to bring it back. He'll have to pay a 20p fine when he does bring it in."

"Hooray!" thought Henry.

"Why don't you call in again next week, and see if it has been returned?" said Miss Purvis.

"Only if you do," said the uniformed attendant, giving Pamela Purvis a wink, "come on your own, eh? No dog-leads, dog-collars, dinosaur fossils or dirty great lumps of rock!"

As Henry walked away from the counter he saw Miss Purvis pick up the big book of *Costume Through the Ages*, and he heard her say to the uniformed attendant: "I've found some lovely Victorian clothes we can copy, Mr Crabtree—who did you say you were going as, in the Grand Procession?"

Library Attendant Colin Crabtree, for such was his full name and title, squared his shoulders, pursed his lips, and looked down from under his peaked cap at Miss Pamela Purvis. "I am dressing up for the occasion, Miss Purvis," he said, "as that well-known Dickensian character, Scrooge."

"Yes," thought Henry, as he walked out through the library doors, "and it suits you too!" But, as before, his thoughts were known to no one but himself.

That same evening, for the first time ever, Henry Hollins took his dinosaur over the back garden fence and into the spinney. At first, the dinosaur showed no

128

objection to being put on a lead—or to wearing a collar. But once inside the spinney, it was a different matter. It was cool and shady and pleasant under the trees, away from the heat of the still-bright evening sun. The prehistoric monster seemed to take a great delight in the darkest corners of the spinney. It thrashed and plunged about, awkwardly, in the ferny undergrowth, dragging Henry along headlong and willy-nilly at the other end of the lead. After a few minutes of this treatment, Henry began to wonder whether he was taking the dinosaur for a walk or whether, in fact, the dinosaur was exercising him?

Henry also started to wonder if he dare let the dinosaur off its lead. Which was obviously what it wanted. Would it stay with him, he wondered, or would it rush off in search of freedom in the wide world beyond the spinney? The young dinosaur had never attempted to escape from the garden it was true, but out here where there was no fence or other boundaries was an entirely different matter.

At last, after being dragged painfully through a bramble bush, Henry decided that he had little choice in the matter. He would have to give the dinosaur its temporary freedom, and hope for the best. Summoning all his strength, he managed to hold the creature in check long enough to slip its collar from the lead.

Immediately, it seemed as if the dinosaur had gone mad with sheer joy. Free from the lead, it lunged off into the thickest part of the spinney where the

129

branches of the trees were entwined overhead, and where the bushes beneath were clumped closely together. Henry watched, half-afraid, as the dinosaur suddenly stood up on its rear legs and, like a toddler taking its first steps, waddled off and disappeared through a patch of tall bracken.

"Hey, boy!" called Henry, running after the dinosaur. "Come back! Heel! Heel!" But there was no sign of the dinosaur, and there was not a sound of it either.

"Crikey," said Henry, glumly. If the monster had charged straight through the spinney and broken out in the clear fields beyond, Henry knew that his days of keeping it a secret were well and truly over.

Henry raced on through the trampled grass and undergrowth, following the path that the dinosaur had plainly taken. He ran into the centre of the spinney and farther, to where the late evening light could be glimpsed through the trees ahead.

"Here, boy! Here, boy!" Henry shouted, then whistled as loudly as he could, and hurried on in search of his prehistoric pet.

Then, to his great relief, as he ran past a giant oak tree, he suddenly came upon the dinosaur. It was standing quite still in the centre of the stream that coursed through the outer edge of the spinney. Henry approached the dinosaur warily, in case it tried to run off again as he drew near. But the dinosaur didn't move, it was standing up on its hind legs, watching Henry calmly, its clumsy back paws splayed out in the stream, obviously enjoying the feel of the running water between its toes.

Again Henry wondered what kind of dinosaur it was. There had been many prehistoric reptiles, he knew, that spent a great deal of their lives living in and near marshes and rivers.

The mighty *Brachiosaurus*, which weighed up to fifty tons and was the heaviest of all dinosaurs, spent most of his time in water. This was because its four legs alone, thick though they might be, were not strong enough to support the huge monster's bulk. Also, the front legs of the *Brachiosaurus* were longer than its back legs. That was how the monster got its name, for *Brachiosaurus* means 'Lizard Arm'. Henry's dinosaur had shorter legs at the front than at the rear. It also seemed as if, when it was fully grown, it was going to spend a lot of time standing up on its rear legs alone, which was something that the *Brachiosaurus* could never do. Not that it needed to, for the *Brachiosaurus* had a long snake-like neck with which it reached up into the tops of trees, or down on to the beds of rivers, for its food. This was true of the *Diplodocus* and the *Brontosaurus* too. Henry's dinosaur had a short, leathery neck, and right at that moment it was trying to reach up to the juicy leaves on the tips of branches by standing upright and supporting itself on its tail.

As Henry walked up to his dinosaur, which was still

standing in the cool, clear stream, it gave up its attempts to nibble at the tree branches and ducked its head beneath the water's surface. It reappeared a moment later, chewing on a mouthful of waterweed.

"I wish I *did* know what you are," said Henry, playfully slapping its thick hide. "I wonder if you know yourself what you are?"

But, of course, the dinosaur made no reply, and chomped steadily on its waterweed.

Henry gave the dinosaur a friendly slap. "Finish up your nice waterweed, old lad," he said, "and we'll be on our way home." The dinosaur gazed at Henry for a moment, blinked, then ducked its head under the stream and emerged with another mouthful of weed. It made no objection at all when, a few minutes later, Henry clipped the lead back on to the collar.

When Henry eventually arrived back at Woodview it was quite dark. He found his mother and father in the sitting-room. They were munching cheese and biscuits and watching an old Hollywood musical film that had been made in black and white on the television.

Fifty or sixty girls, with big bows on their shoes, were tap-dancing energetically on top of fifty or sixty snow-white pianos while a man with shiny, black hair sang a song about "June" and "moon" and "honey-love" and "turtle-dove".

Mrs Hollins was enjoying the film hugely, but her husband was plainly bored by it. He looked round, grumpily, and frowned as Henry entered the sitting-room.

"Where have you been till this time, son?" Albert demanded.

"Why?" asked Henry. "I'm not late, am I?"

"Late? *Late!*" and Albert Hollins almost exploded as he spat out the words. "I'll say you're late! You're supposed to go to bed after the space-ship programme finishes. That was I-don't-know-how-long-since. There's been a variety programme on; there's been an American detective programme on; *and* there's been a documentary programme on about king penguins—that's how late you are, Henry—three programmes late!"

"Where have you *been*, Henry?" asked Emily, tearing herself away from the television and the musical film.

"Only down to the bottom of the garden."

"If you ask me," said Albert sternly, "you spend too much time down the bottom of that garden, larking about in my shed."

"Yes, Dad," said Henry, meekly.

"Well, it's going to stop . . ." said Albert.

"Yes, Dad," said Henry again.

". . . And no messing," said Albert. "You can just clear all them books and rocks and rubbish and things out of that shed tomorrow."

"Tomorrow?" echoed Henry, horrified.

"You heard—tomorrow. I want that garden shed

133

for a specific purpose," his father said. "I've got some painting to do."

"Oh," said Henry, dumbly.

"So don't forget," said Albert, and then: "Go on, now—off you go to bed. G'night."

"Goodnight, Dad. Goodnight, Mum," said Henry, making his way to the door.

"Goodnight, Henry," said his mother, dragging her eyes from the TV set once again, briefly, then turning back.

As Henry went out into the hall he caught a last glimpse, on the telly, of the fifty or sixty girls. They were now dressed in clogs and shawls and were dancing round a giant windmill while the man with the black, shiny hair sang a song about "two lips" and "tulips" and "Amsterdam" and "how-in-love-I-am".

Henry closed the sitting-room door, softly, and went upstairs.

Some time later, lying in bed with his arms behind his head, Henry gave some serious thought to his dinosaur. He came to the opinion that things were not as bad as they had at first seemed. The dinosaur was growing too big for the garden shed anyway. He would have had to move it sooner or later. His father's demand that he clear out the garden shed tomorrow had only moved forward the inevitable day. Perhaps, thought Henry, he could move the dinosaur into the spinney permanently? The creature had seemed more than contented down there, and had shown not the slightest desire to move out from the shelter of the trees into the open country. And the spinney was quite secluded, opening as it did on to fallow farmland. Nobody ever went near the place. At any rate, it was worth a try—and he certainly couldn't think of anywhere else to move it. Yes, Henry decided, he would take the dinosaur down to the spinney the following evening and leave it there—and just hope for the best.

And, having made his decision, Henry closed his eyes and was soon fast asleep.

Down in the sitting-room, the Hollywood musical came to an end as the man with the black, shiny hair put his arms around a lady with long eyelashes and tight, blond curls, while the fifty or sixty girls danced round them to an upsurge of violin music.

"They don't make films like that any longer," said Emily Hollins with deep satisfaction, and she leant forward and switched off the television set. Then, remembering what had been said earlier, she turned to her husband: "I do think you were a bit harsh on our Henry," she said. "Making him clear all of his things out of that garden shed, you know how much he enjoys himself playing down there."

"He's been getting a bit too secretive, if you ask me, has that boy, of late," said Albert. "Besides I *do* need it myself. Like I said—I've got some painting to do."

"What sort of painting?"

"I've got to paint a big plaster statue of Oliver Twist," said Albert, proudly.

"You haven't!"

"I have!"

"Well I never!" said Emily, impressed.

"It's for the factory," explained Albert. "You know the Grand Procession they're having through the town centre in Dickens Week?"

"Yes?"

"Well, the factory's going to enter a decorated float this year, on the back of a lorry. It's going to have a plaster Oliver Twist on it, asking for more."

"My word," said Emily, "that'll be something to look out for then, in the procession."

Albert smiled, a sort of secret smile, before he spoke again. "I'll tell you something else you can watch out for in the procession this year, as well."

"What's that?" said Emily.

"Guess who's going to drive our factory lorry?"

"I've no idea," said Emily.

"I'll give you a clue then," said Albert. "He's sitting not very far from you right at this minute."

Emily clapped her hands together in surprise. "Not you!" she exclaimed.

"I am," said Albert. "I was invited personally by Mr Grimsdyke, the head of Garden Gnomes, to perform the task."

"Fame at last!" said Emily.

"Anyway," said Albert, "as they're a bit behind in

making the plaster figures for the float, I said I'd give them a hand and paint the Oliver Twist one myself. I thought I'd do it in the garden shed."

Emily nodded, approvingly, and then she looked thoughtful. "What's it going to be doing?" she said.

"What's what going to be doing?"

"Your Oliver Twist statue. What position will it be taking up?"

"Oh!" Albert's brow cleared. "Why, it'll be holding its bowl out of course—asking for more."

"I don't suppose," suggested Emily, "that you could give it a collecting-box to hold instead? I'm *so* behind in my door-to-door collection on behalf of Our Feathered and Furry Friends—"

But Albert Hollins was shaking his head, firmly. "It's got to be a gruel bowl," he said. "It would make nonsense of Charles Dickens if there was a statue of Oliver Twist collecting on behalf of Our Feathered and Furry Friends."

Emily sighed and nodded, forced to agree that there was some truth in what Albert said. And then she suddenly smiled. "I know!" she said. "I think I'll write to Uncle George and Auntie Gertie, and ask them down to stay for the weekend of the Grand Procession. They'd enjoy watching you drive that float."

"Why not?" said Albert. "You do that thing."

"It would give them something to think about," said Emily. "You know how they're always boasting about their son Cyril who went off to be a lumberjack in Canada."

"Don't I just," said Albert, gloomily.

Emily smiled again. "I shall feel *so* proud of you, Albert. Won't you feel proud? I should think you'll really enjoy yourself behind the wheel of that float."

"Oh, I don't know so much," said Albert, modestly. "It's all nose-to-tail stuff, is procession driving. One mile an hour all the way. You know me—I do like to get my foot down." He paused and frowned before continuing: "One mile an hour, nose-to-tail—it'll be just like driving in a continual boring traffic jam!"

# 10

Henry Hollins studied the picture in the *Illustrated Encyclopedia of Dinosaurs*, and then he rolled over in the grass and studied his pet. There was no doubt about it, he decided, they were one and the same.

"That's what you are, then," said Henry. "You're an *Anatosaurus.*"

The dinosaur gave no sign whatsoever that it was either pleased or displeased at hearing of its true identity, but it went on nibbling at the weeds underneath the stream, contentedly.

"Don't you want to hear about yourself?" said Henry. "It's all written down in here; I've just got it from the library." And he rolled back on to his stomach and read out the words that were written under the picture of the dinosaur.

*The* Anatosaurus *was a member of the duck-billed dinosaur family that lived during the Cretaceous Period, one hundred and twenty million years ago. The* Anatosaurus *was a strong swimmer and spent its life along the shore of great swamps and seas. Its diet consisted mostly of water-plants which it chewed on with its thousands and thousands of teeth that grew in countless rows on both its upper and lower jaws.*

*The* Anatosaurus *was a harmless and, generally, a*

*clumsy slow-moving creature, but it could, in fact, move*
*quickly when in flight from one of its natural enemies, the*
*meat-eating dinosaurs. The* Anatosaurus *was one of the*
*largest of the duck-billed dinosaurs, and averaged over ten*
*metres in length.*

"There you are," said Henry, turning back to his
dinosaur. "That's you—an *Anatosaurus.*" The dinosaur ducked its head beneath the surface of the
stream again and, again, came up with another
mouthful of weed. "I think", Henry went on, "I'll call
you Nat. What do you think of that for a name?" As
though in answer, the dinosaur lowered its head and
cocked a leathery ear on one side, allowing Henry to
scratch its head. Henry Hollins and the *Anatosaurus*
were firm friends.

The summer was slipping by. The end of the school
term had arrived and gone and Henry Hollins had
already enjoyed two weeks of warm and splendid
holiday. The dinosaur had been living in the spinney
now for almost two months, and Henry was only
surprised at how simple it had all proved.

Unaware of the dinosaur's existence, the citizens of
Staplewood had given it no cause for concern and, in
return, the dinosaur had done nothing in any way to
bother the citizens of Staplewood. In all this time, in
fact, the dinosaur had seemed more than content to
stay close by the stream and the centre of the wood,
rarely venturing within a score of yards of the edge of
the trees; perfectly happy to nibble all day and every

day at the sweet, green leaves on the overhanging branches, or to chew placidly at the many and varied plants and weeds that grew alongside and under the running water.

And, every day without exception, Henry Hollins had climbed over the fence at the bottom of the garden, and joined his prehistoric pal in that leafy surround where they had spent the mornings, afternoons and evenings in peaceful contentment. Sometimes they frolicked, sometimes they played hide-and-seek, but more often than not they lounged and lazed away the hours on the shady banks of the stream where, true to the description in the *Encyclopedia of Dinosaurs,* the *Anatosaurus* ate, and ate—and grew, and grew, and grew.

Henry's dinosaur was now big enough for him to clamber up its broad-beamed back and sit quite comfortably perched up behind its head, his legs dangling over its shoulders. And, too, it seemed as if the dinosaur was more than happy to have Henry up there. Then, with the boy's hands clutching tightly around the top of the monster's bony head, the *Anatosaurus* would lurch off, leaning slightly forward, lumbering excitedly between the trees on its thick back legs, occasionally steadying itself to turn a corner with its broad, strong tail.

Henry and the *Anatosaurus* passed many a carefree summer day, joyfully and undisturbed. Although, it would not be true to say that no other person ever

141

ventured into the spinney during those early weeks of August.

Occasionally a courting couple would stroll through the trees, hand in hand, walking in at one end of the spinney and out at the other. Sometimes a handful of hikers would stride purposefully through the wood, bent forward, their rucksacks high up on their backs. And on three separate occasions the farmer who owned the land had sauntered through the trees, his shotgun under his arm, his eyes peering into the undergrowth in search of rabbits. But not one of these visitors to the spinney had caught sight of the dinosaur. Their minds had been on other things: the farmer's on his rabbits; the hikers' on the path ahead; the courting couple's thoughts were on each other.

There had been one particular day though, when Henry and his dinosaur had had their narrowest escape of all, and that was on the afternoon when the coach-load of American tourists had come to Staple-wood.

One warm Wednesday afternoon a chromium-gleaming coach had pulled up at a layby on the bypass road, some few hundred yards across the fields away from the spinney. The coach door had swung open and the coach-load of American tourists had tumbled out, chattering excitedly, for a breath of fresh air and to take in the scenery.

The American men tourists all smoked fat cigars

142

and wore shirts with palm trees on them outside their trousers. The American lady tourists all wore sun-glasses decorated with imitation diamonds and they carried shopping baskets with pictures of William Shakespeare on the sides, which they had bought in their last stopping-place, Stratford-on-Avon. All of the American tourists had at least two cameras slung round their necks. The tour guide, a tall thin man called Ernest Groves, had pointed across the fields to where Staplewood lay spread out below them, like a far-off model village.

"Ladies and gentlemen," said Ernest Groves, "you see before you the ancient town of Staplewood, which is steeped in literary history, where that renowned author, Charles Dickens, wrote some of his world-famous and much-loved novels."

"Gosh," had said one American tourist.

Then, "Gee," another had said.

And, "Which of his novels?" a third American tourist had asked. This third tourist was a lady from Michigan, whose name was Evangeline Cheezburger, and who was by far the most inquisitive tourist in the party.

"Quite a number of them," Mr Groves had replied, untruthfully, for he didn't know the answer. Then, not wishing to disappoint Miss Cheezburger, he had added: "Most of them, in fact."

"Wow," had said one American tourist.

"Well, wadderyerknow?" another one had said.

143

Evangeline Cheezburger had not replied for several moments. She had been too busy drinking in the countryside. Then, all at once, she had clapped her hands, crowed with delight, and pointed off across the fields at the spinney. "Say!" she had said. "Will you just look at that cute little teensy-weensy forest!"

"That, ma'am," Ernest Groves had replied, "is what we in England call a copse or spinney."

"You don't say?" Miss Cheezburger had replied. "I'll sure bet your Mr Dickens filled up a heck of a lot of notebooks in all *that* peace and quiet!"

"Indeed he did, ma'am," Mr Groves had said, making things up as he went along. "Why, he wrote twenty chapters of *Barnaby Rudge* in that there spinney—and the *whole* of *Pickwick Papers!*"

"You don't say?" Miss Cheezburger had said again, wringing her hands in sheer delight. "Well, one thing's for sure," she continued, "I must have a couple of snapshots of that old spinney to show the folks back home!" And so saying, she had leapt over the dry-stone wall and had set off, running across the fallow field beyond which lay the spinney.

"Come back at once, ma'am!" Mr Groves had yelled after her. "We haven't time to stop for photographs! We have to press on as far as the birthplace of the Brontë sisters by tea-time!"

But it had been too late. Miss Evangeline Cheezburger had already got half-way across the field and was out of earshot.

As she drew closer to the spinney, Miss Cheez-burger had slowed down her pace. She had stopped running partly because she was out of breath, and partly because it had occurred to her that a photo-graph of a group of trees wasn't going to be all that exciting as she had first thought. But Evangeline Cheezburger was a determined lady, and she cer-tainly wasn't going to go back to the coach without *something* in her camera to show for her run across the fields. Perhaps, she thought, if she went quietly, she might come across some kind of English wildlife worth recording? A family of ear-pricked, nose-twitching bunnies, say, or a whole nestful of baby thrushes poking their hungry beaks up at the sky?

Evangeline Cheezburger had raised her camera to the at-the-ready position, and had tiptoed into the spinney, ducking quietly from bush to tree trunk, from tree trunk to bush.

At the same time that Miss Cheezburger had made her intrepid trek into darkest England, Henry Hollins and his *Anatosaurus* had been enjoying a game of hide-and-seek. It had been Henry's turn to hide, and the task of the dinosaur to go and seek. Hearing the crackle and snap of twigs from behind a blackberry bush, the *Anatosaurus* had padded towards it. At that same moment, Evangeline Cheezburger, behind the blackberry bush, had listened to the sound of approaching padded feet from the other side, placed her finger on the camera button and had held

145

her breath. She was not sure of all the varieties of wildlife that were to be found in England, but this one certainly sounded like one of the largest kind.

The *Anatosaurus* had loomed up over the top of the blackberry bush at the very moment that Miss Cheezburger had popped her head up on her side. It was difficult to tell, in the excitement of the moment, which of the two, the prehistoric monster or the Michigan lady, was the most surprised. The *Anatosaurus* snuffled and snorted and reared up its head in horror. Miss Evangeline Cheezburger screamed and howled and her mouth dropped open in astonishment. And then, as one, they both turned and fled in opposite directions. To Miss Cheezburger's credit though, she had the presence of mind to press home the camera-shutter button at the very second that she stared into the monster's leathery face.

Back at the coach, the party of American tourists had watched, amazed, as their companion sprinted back towards them across the fields in headlong terror-stricken flight.

"I've seen it! I've seen it!" Evangeline had cried as she drew near. "I've seen it with my very own two eyes!"

"Seen what, ma'am?" Ernest Groves had asked, offering her a hand over the dry-stone wall.

"Why, the Loch Ness monster, you limey goop!" Miss Cheezburger had replied, pushing his offer of a helping hand aside. And as she struggled over the wall unaided, the party of American tourists had clustered around her, some of them displaying excitement and others showing concern.

"Where is it, Evangeline?" said one.

"What does it look like?" said another.

"Let's get out of here!" a third one had cried.

But Ernest Groves had brought order and sanity back to the proceedings by firmly shaking his head and raising his voice above the rest. "Whatever you saw, ma'am, I can assure you that it was no Loch Ness monster, not in *this* part of the United Kingdom."

"I know what I saw—I was there!" Evangeline had yelled, verging on hysteria. "It came up at me over a blackberry bush. And it had an ugly monster head and a long, green monster tail. It was the Loch Ness monster I've seen at home, back in Michigan, on the Come To Britain posters!"

"Ah," Ernest Groves had said, raising a forefinger in the air. "And there you have it, ma'am. Britain, yes; England, no. The Loch Ness monster is a native of Scotland. There are no monsters to be found in the English countryside. And I've been a registered guide for seventeen years so I should know."

"For pete's sake," the excitable Miss Cheezburger had cried, "I saw the gosh-darned creature with my own eyes!"

Again Ernest Groves had shaken his head, gently but firmly. "Ghosts and ghouls we have in plenty, but monsters—no. Some folks say 'more's the pity', but speaking for myself, I think it's a good job we're without them in this country. I can't bear monsters, nasty, snarling, great things. Give me a nice, friendly ghost any day of the week. As a matter of fact, we're due to visit a castle tomorrow that's haunted by a headless ghost—but at this rate, we'll never get there! Please, ma'am, I must ask you to board the coach!"

"Have it your own way, but I *did* see that monster, and I'll prove it to you too," Evangeline Cheezburger had snapped back, holding up her camera. "There's a photograph of it in here!"

Ernest Groves permitted a knowing little smile to flit across his face. "You'll pardon me contradicting you again, ma'am," he had said. "But if you used that camera with the lens cap on, I very much doubt that you'll find any sort of photograph in there—monster or otherwise."

And Evangeline Cheezburger had looked down at her camera and had seen, to her disappointment, that she had indeed forgotten to take off the lens cap when she had taken the photograph. There was no way of proving now that the monster did exist.

"Wait!" she had said, appealing to her fellow tourists. "Come back with me now into that spinney—it isn't very big, and the monster's enormous—we'll soon find it."

The party of American tourists hesitated.

"All aboard!" cried Ernest Groves. "Resume your seats, please, for the remainder of this wonderful

149

coach tour! The Brontë country this afternoon *and* a haunted castle tomorrow morning!"

And, one by one, the American tourists had drifted across and got back on to the coach. At last, only Evangeline Cheezburger and Ernest Groves were left standing by the dry-stone wall.

"Well, ma'am," Ernest Groves had said, politely, "are you joining the party, or shall we leave you behind?"

Sadly, and with more than one backward glance, Miss Evangeline Cheezburger had walked across and climbed on to the coach. Ernest Groves was the last person to board. He pressed a button and the chromium-gleaming door slid shut without a sound.

The coach pulled out of the layby, out into the bypass road, and off in search of other excitements.

Henry Hollins had sighed with relief as he watched the tourist coach drive away. He got to his feet in his hiding-place close by the edge of the spinney, and had kept on watching until the coach carrying the Americans was no more than a bright, shining speck of reflected sunlight on the far horizon.

The afternoon of the American tourists had been the closest shave that he and the dinosaur had ever had, thought Henry, as he picked his *Encyclopedia of Dinosaurs* up off the grass and tucked it under his arm. The sun was dipping down behind the topmost branches of a copper beech, and another day was almost over.

"G'night, Nat," Henry called cheerfully, waving across the stream at his dinosaur that was grazing contentedly on the opposite bank.

The *Anatosaurus* splashed towards Henry through the water, with the usual tangled network of plant and weed trailing from its mouth. The dinosaur lowered its head and nudged the boy in the chest, gently, wanting him to scratch its head.

"I knew you when you only wanted your tummy tickled," said Henry, rubbing hard with his knuckles on the monster's bony skull. "But you're a bit too big for that now."

The *Anatosaurus* grunted, softly, then turned, and Henry gave its broad beam a friendly slap. As the dinosaur ambled back towards its favourite patch, Henry called after it, "See you tomorrow!" Then he, too, turned and strode off, through the spinney, towards his home.

# I I

Albert Hollins was busy outside the garden shed when Henry climbed over the garden fence on his way back from the spinney. "Hey up!" shouted Albert, glancing at his watch. "Where've you been hiding yourself this time?"

"Only down in the spinney," said Henry.

"You want to keep out of there, that's private property, you know," said Albert.

"I wasn't doing any harm," said Henry.

"No," grumbled Albert, "and I don't suppose you were up to any good either. It's a pity you can't find something to do that will keep you *usefully* occupied—I know I can."

As Henry walked across the bottom end of the garden, up through the vegetable patch, Albert Hollins returned to his task. Albert had brought a large plaster statue of a small boy out of the garden shed. He had painted the statue inside the shed, and was now filling in the finer details with a camel-hair brush.

The statue was wearing blue painted knee-breeches and a yellow painted, open-necked shirt. It was holding a painted wooden bowl in both hands, and its head was tilted upwards as though the boy was pleading with someone. The statue also had bare feet which were painted a bright red, as were its hands and face.

Albert Hollins stepped back, proudly, and admired his handiwork as Henry joined him by the garden shed. "I'll bet you can't guess who that is?" said Albert.

"Oliver Twist," said Henry.

"That's right," admitted Albert. "He's holding up his gruel bowl, asking for more. He's going on the back of the factory float, you know, in the Grand Procession on Saturday. I'm driving it."

"I know," said Henry, "Mum told me." Henry studied the statue, puzzled, and then continued: "Why are his hands and face and feet all red? Is he supposed to be sunburnt?"

"Of course not!" Albert snapped. "They're not supposed to be red—they're supposed to be flesh-coloured. Only I couldn't get any flesh-coloured paint." Albert paused and walked round the statue, slowly. "He doesn't look *too* red, does he?" he said at last, anxiously.

"Well . . ." said Henry.

"Anyway," said Albert, "I don't suppose anybody will notice when he's stuck up on top of the float. He only looks red to you because you're standing close to him."

"You could be right," said Henry, and he went on his way up the garden path.

"And just you mind your manners when you get into that house!" Albert called after his son. "Uncle George and Auntie Gertie have arrived, so behave yourself for the next few days; don't show us up!"

Henry groaned inwardly at the thought of Uncle George and Auntie Gertie as he pushed open the kitchen door.

Emily Hollins, Uncle George and Auntie Gertie were sitting looking at each other, all three perched politely on the edge of chairs, when Henry walked into the sitting-room. Auntie Gertie was commanding the conversation, as was usually the case, and Uncle George was agreeing with her every word, as he always did. Emily Hollins was smiling distantly, casting occasional glances at the television set which was switched off, and wondering if she was missing any interesting programmes.

"Oh, dear me!" said Auntie Gertie as Henry entered, "your Henry doesn't seem to put much weight on, does he?"

"He doesn't," agreed Uncle George. "He'll never be heavy-weight champion of the world, that's for certain."

"He's all right," said Emily, slipping an elastic band round two hundred and fifty *Brown Windsor* soup-tin labels. "He's only young yet."

"When our Cyril was his age," said Auntie Gertie, "he was like the side of a house."

"Like a barn door," agreed Uncle George.

"Yes, but our Henry's not like your Cyril, is he?" said Emily.

"There's *nobody* like our Cyril, he's one on his own—one in a million," said Auntie Gertie. "You ought to see the letter we had from him last week, I'll read it to you later on. He's doing ever so well in Canada. Your Henry could do with taking a leaf out of our Cyril's book."

"That's right," agreed Uncle George. "He could use our Cyril as an example."

"Perhaps our Henry doesn't *want* to be a lumberjack," said Emily.

"He isn't just a lumberjack, our Cyril," said Auntie Gertie, "he's got promoted."

"It's true," agreed Uncle George. "He's been put in charge of a whole forest!"

"He'll end up being made the president of Canada before he's finished, will our Cyril," said Auntie Gertie, proudly.

"They don't have a president in Canada," said Henry. "They have a prime minister, like we do."

Auntie Gertie frowned, and glared at Henry. "They *will* have a president before long," she said, "if our Cyril has anything to do with it."

"What do you want to be when you grow up?" said Uncle George to Henry.

"A palaeontologist," said Henry.

"Humph," grunted Auntie Gertie, who didn't want

to own up that she didn't know what a palaeontologist was.

But at least Uncle George wasn't ashamed to admit his ignorance. "What the hummers is one of them?" he asked.

"A man who studies dinosaurs and other prehistoric reptiles," said Henry.

"*Dinosaurs?*" said Auntie Gertie. "They're a bit old-fashioned, aren't they?"

"I should say so," said Uncle George. "They were before the ark, were dinosaurs."

"Oooh," said Auntie Gertie, wriggling her shoulders, disapprovingly, "you want to look to the future, Henry, like our Cyril. I mean, take going to Canada—Canada's the country of the future."

Just then, before Henry could reply, Albert entered, wiping paint from his hands with a piece of turpentiny rag. "Well," he announced, "that's Oliver Twist all poshed up and ready!"

"Oliver Twist?" said Auntie Gertie.

"Albert's driving a float in the Grand Procession on Saturday," said Emily proudly. "It's going to have a big Oliver Twist on the back of it!"

"Holding his bowl out and asking for more," said Albert.

Auntie Gertie sniffed. "It's easy to see where your Henry gets his old-fashioned ideas from," she said. "Oliver Twist indeed!"

156

"I thought Oliver Twist went out with Charles Dickens," said Uncle George.

"We thought you'd *like* to see the procession," said Emily. "We thought you'd *enjoy* it. That's why we asked you down. There's going to be lots of decorated floats, and dozens of folk dressed up in those Victorian costumes. We *thought* it would be right up your street."

Auntie Gertie pulled a long face. "I suppose we can go and see it, if there's nothing better to do. But I must say, I'd much more rather have preferred to see something a bit more modern!"

"And me," agreed Uncle George. "Our Cyril collects foreign stamps with astronauts and cosmonauts on them," he added.

"It isn't all old-fashioned, you know," said Albert Hollins defensively. "There's going to be a flypast of RAF fighter jets before the Grand Procession, *and* there's a display of pot-plants, cacti and succulents in the Civic Hall."

Auntie Gertie sniffed again. "I suppose it will help pass the Saturday afternoon on," was all she said.

Two colourful banners were stretched across Staplewood High Street: DICKENS WEEK Aug. 18th-24th!! read the first, and: GRAND PROCESSION ON SATURDAY Aug. 23rd!! announced the second.

There were also great lengths of bunting hanging on both sides of the High Street, from the Electricity

157

Showrooms at one end down as far as the Bingo Hall at the other. Then, from on top of each and every concrete lamp-post there beamed down the cheery face of a plastic Mr Pickwick and, across the imposing Georgian frontage of the Staplewood Town Hall, there hung an enormous banner that carried a giant picture of Charles Dickens himself.

Although the procession had not yet started—it was in fact assembling at that moment in the civic car park behind the larger of the two supermarkets—already both sides of the High Street were thronged with excited crowds packed together and all in holiday mood. Temporary barriers had been erected the night before to hold back the throng and, spaced out in front of the barriers, stood a score or so of genial policemen, each one of whom was looking forward himself to the treat that lay ahead.

Packed in the crowd, in the centre of the High Street outside the Pig and Bucket Hotel, stood Emily and Henry Hollins and Uncle George and Auntie Gertie.

Henry had had to forsake his friend, the *Anatosaurus,* for the afternoon, in order to come and watch the Grand Procession. Not that Henry minded all that much, for he quite enjoyed watching processions, and he knew the dinosaur would be all right on its own for a while. There was no chance of it being discovered for the entire population of Staplewood was packed along the High Street. All the same, Henry was just a little sad because he couldn't bring the *Anatosaurus* along with him to see the procession.

Auntie Gertie, however, did not seem to be enjoying herself at all. She was becoming angry because the procession was a couple of minutes late in starting. Auntie Gertie leant over the barrier, irritably, and looked first one way up the High Street and then down the other.

"What time do you make it, George?" she said. But when Uncle George looked at his watch he found that it had stopped, and that made Auntie Gertie more cross than ever. She tapped a policeman on the shoulder with her umbrella and said, "Excuse me, Constable, but do you know how long this procession is going to be?"

The policeman stroked his chin, smiled, and made a joke. "About three quarters of a mile, madam," he said.

"Don't try to be funny with me!" snapped Auntie Gertie, and then she said in a loud voice for the benefit of anyone who cared to listen, "My son, Cyril, who's a lumberjack, says the Canadian Mounted Police are *much* more polite than English policemen!"

"Hush, Auntie Gertie!" whispered Emily Hollins; and even Uncle George shuffled his feet with embarrassment and looked the other way.

Luckily, however, nobody in the crowd was paying any attention to Auntie Gertie at that moment, for there was an air of growing excitement as the word spread along the High Street that the Grand Procession was about to start. Henry Hollins leant over the barrier and gazed along the empty road. Although he could not see any sign yet of the decorated floats, he did see two people that he recognized.

Angus McGillicuddy, the chief photographer on the *Staplewood Guardian*, was standing in the middle of the High Street, holding his camera and looking important. With him was the junior reporter who had interviewed Henry about his fossil all those weeks before. The junior reporter was now waiting to cover the story of the Grand Procession for the local paper. Angus McGillicuddy was waiting to take a photograph, for the front page, of his editor-in-chief who, dressed up as Mr Micawber, was taking part in the Grand Procession. Both of the newspapermen were looking up the High Street towards the civic car park where, at that moment, the procession was forming up, ready for the word to move off.

Standing at the entrance to the car park, Police Superintendent Reginald Farrington gripped his megaphone tightly. He was keenly aware of the responsibility that lay on his shoulders, for it was his duty to give the Grand Procession the word to go. At the head of the parade stood the Staplewood Brass Band, dressed in the costumes of Victorian musicians, tuning their instruments, impatient for the off.

Immediately behind the Brass Band, at the wheel of his factory's decorated lorry, Albert Hollins licked

his lips, anxiously. Albert's float had been chosen to lead off the parade and the honour was making him nervous. He was suffering from butterflies in his stomach, and he wished the procession would start.

Behind the plaster-gnome factory's lorry, where the red-faced Oliver Twist gazed up at the sky, stood a group of children from Henry's school. They were dressed up as Dickensian orphans, and they all carried wooden gruel bowls. The children were under the eagle-eyed supervision of the lanky hook-nosed English teacher, Nigel Popplewell, who was dressed as Mr Bumble the Beadle. Nigel Popplewell was raging at the top of his voice, trying to get his orphans into line.

"You there!" shouted Mr Popplewell at the ginger-headed Rory Stigwood. "Get into line, boy, before you feel my hand across your ear!"

"Please, sir!" the unhappy Stigwood called back. "I'm not supposed to be an orphan, sir, I'm supposed to be the Artful Dodger, sir!"

"Then who are you supposed to be with?" screamed Mr Popplewell.

"The assistant headmaster, sir," called Stigwood. "He's dressed up as Fagin, sir!"

"Then go and find him, Stigwood!" bellowed Mr Popplewell. "And stop hanging round my orphan boys!"

Stigwood, alias the Artful Dodger, scampered away

in search of the assistant headmaster, alias the scoundrel Fagin.

Behind the orphan boys came another float, provided by the Gas Showrooms and decorated to represent Bob Cratchit's home on Christmas day.

Behind the Gas Showrooms' decorated float stood Pamela Purvis, the librarian, with the editor-in-chief of the *Staplewood Guardian*, and these two were dressed as Mr and Mrs Micawber. They were accompanied by Mr Crabtree, the library attendant, who was got up as the miser, Ebenezer Scrooge.

And behind this trio came another float, and then more dressed-up people, and then another float; and so the parade went on, line after line, across the civic car park, waiting for the off.

Police Superintendent Farrington lifted his megaphone to his mouth. "Silence, everybody!" he shouted, and a curious, quiet stillness fell on the massed ranks. The police officer cocked his head on one side and waited—and listened.

And there came, from overhead, a growing, whining, roaring sound.

"nnniiiaaaeeeooo*OOOWWWWWW!!!*"

It was the scream of jet engines from the RAF fighters as the planes dived low and shot across the town, dipping their wings as they sped low along the High Street.

"Hooray! Hooray!" yelled the eager crowd from behind the barriers.

"Now!" yelled Police Superintendent Farrington into his megaphone.

"One—two—three—four!" cried the leader of the Staplewood Brass Band, putting his right foot forward.

"Off we go then," muttered Albert Hollins nervously, and he released his handbrake.

The Grand Procession moved out into the High Street.

"*NNNIIIIIIiiiaaaeeeoooowwwww.*"

The whine of the jet engines faded away as the RAF fighters swung off across the town.

"Hooray! Hooray!" cried the joyful crowds from behind the barriers as the Victorian Brass Band led the parade out into the High Street, trumpets blowing, cymbals clashing. The Grand Procession was underway at last.

"nnniiiaaaeeeooo*OOOWWWWWW!!!* "

Beyond the town, the high-pitched sound of jet engines screamed across the quiet of the spinney as the RAF planes, still zooming low, raced over the tips of the trees on their way across the countryside and left Staplewood behind.

"*NNNIIIAAAEEEOOOOOOWWWWWW!!*"

The *Anatosaurus,* chomping lazily at a patch of duckweed, reared up instantly on its hind legs, stood stock-still for several seconds, petrified with fright, before it threw back its flat bony head and let out a terrifying cry that all but drowned the fading roar of the jet engines.

And then the *Anatosaurus*, suffering a fear that stretched beyond the comprehension of its prehistoric mind, took to its thick and sturdy back legs and fled in panic through the trees. The dinosaur, in headlong flight now and heedless of the spinney's shelter, broke from cover and hurtled across the uneven fallow fields in the direction of the town.

In the High Street, the long procession was threading its way out of the civic car park and slowly moving in rumbustious file, cheered on by the crowds on either side, with the Staplewood Brass Band panting and blowing to the fore.

"There he is!" said Emily Hollins to her son. "There's your dad's float, Henry—give him a wave!"

Henry waved.

"Why is his Oliver Twist all red in the face?" asked Auntie Gertie.

"He was sunburnt in the book, Auntie Gertie, didn't you know?" said Henry, hiding a smile.

And Auntie Gertie did one of her sniffs, not knowing whether or not Henry was joking, but not wishing to show her ignorance.

Henry's secret smile, however, froze on his lips. A thousand voices had risen as one in a long, loud scream. Following the noise, Henry looked along the High Street in the opposite direction to the procession. The *Anatosaurus*, in lumbering, clumsy but yet

165

speedy flight, was heading full-tilt for the Grand Procession and the Staplewood Brass Band. The scream was taken up all along the High Street, on both sides, as the dinosaur continued on its careering path towards the oncoming parade.

"Oh, gosh," thought Henry glumly.

Emily Hollins' lower jaw dropped open as she stared in wide-eyed wonder.

Uncle George gulped and cleared his throat quickly, twice.

"Well," announced Auntie Gertie, unimpressed, and believing it all to be part of the afternoon's show, "if this is what they call family entertainment, give me the telly anytime!"

The Staplewood Brass Band, suddenly aware of the charging dinosaur, threw down its instruments and ran off, leaping over the barriers to join the fast dispersing crowds. Albert Hollins, behind the steering-wheel of the first decorated float, slammed on his brakes as the *Anatosaurus* loomed up in his path. The lorry pulled up with a jerk and the plaster Oliver Twist toppled off the back and smashed into a thousand pieces on the road. The workhouse orphans scattered in all directions, throwing down their wooden gruel bowls. The bowls rolled off down the High Street, and Dickensian characters of all shapes and sizes tripped over them. Mr Bumble the Beadle fell down and burst his nose. Mrs Micawber slipped and rolled in the gutter, her skirts flying. Mr

Micawber collided with Jacob Marley's Ghost whose chains broke apart and rattled all over the pavement. The Ghost-of-Christmas-Past tripped over a gruel bowl and fell against Sergeant Buzfuz who, in order to save himself from falling, grabbed at the scoundrel Fagin and all three of them tumbled to the ground. Tall Victorian top-hats were everywhere; bonnets and muffs littered the ground. Lorries crashed through the temporary barriers; decorated floats mounted the pavement and drove into lamp-posts bringing plastic heads of Mr Pickwick to the ground.

Never before had devastation like it been seen in Staplewood. The *Anatosaurus*, which had stopped dead in its tracks, sat down and watched the goings-on with keen interest.

"Come on," said Emily Hollins, grabbing Henry firmly by the hand, "we're going home."

The same idea was shared by everybody who had gone into the centre of Staplewood that afternoon, both spectators and members of the procession alike. Within five minutes of the dinosaur appearing, the High Street cleared like magic. All that remained was debris, empty lorries, the *Anatosaurus* and one policeman.

It was the same policeman who had spoken to Auntie Gertie. He walked up, slowly, to face the dinosaur which was now nibbling at some artificial grass that had been part of a tableau on one of the floats. The dinosaur looked across at the policeman with half a yard of plastic grass dangling from its mouth.

"Oi, ugly," said the policeman. "Scarper."

The dinosaur didn't move, although it did stop chewing for a couple of seconds.

The policeman took out his truncheon and waggled it in the dinosaur's face, threateningly. "You heard me!" he said. "Hop it!"

The *Anatosaurus* could not understand what the policeman was saying, but it seemed as if it gathered what he wanted from the severe tone of his voice. It stumbled up on to its feet, turned, and lolloped off, peaceably, down the High Street, back the way it had come.

The policeman watched it go and then he picked his way through the debris to a public telephone box. He opened the door, went in, lifted the receiver and dialled 999.

"Emergency?" said the operator. "Which service do you require: Police, Ambulance or Fire Brigade?"

The policeman studied the damage through the window before he spoke, and then: "All of them," he said.

## 12

Albert and Emily Hollins, and Uncle George and Auntie Gertie, were in the sitting-room at Woodview, ruminating on the afternoon's happenings. Henry was also present, but he was keeping his own knowledge of the affair to himself.

"Well, I don't know *what* to make of it," said Albert, for the umpteenth time, rhythmically stirring the cup of hot, sweet tea that Emily had made for him, to combat his mild attack of shock.

"I don't know either, dear," said Emily, as she watched her husband sip his hot tea, and then she added, "I've just remembered one thing I *must* do—and that's go out selling flags next Saturday for the St John's Ambulance Brigade."

"It makes you wonder what this country's coming to," said Auntie Gertie. "Letting a great, big, horrible thing like that roam loose on the streets!"

"That's right," agreed Uncle George.

"They wouldn't allow it to happen in Canada," said Auntie Gertie.

"They certainly would not," said Uncle George.

"They're very strict in Canada about that sort of thing," said Auntie Gertie. "They wouldn't give it house room there."

"What puzzles me," said Emily, "is what it was?"

"That's what puzzles all of us," said Albert, and then glancing up at the clock on the mantelpiece, he added: "Why not switch the telly on, and see if they say anything about it on the news?"

"Oh, yes!" said Emily. "Now that *is* a good idea. You switch it on, Henry, you're the nearest."

Henry did as he had been told.

The news was half-way through, and the news-reader was looking very solemn and talking about the cricket match that was taking place between Australia and England. When he came to the end of the sports item however, he smiled as he picked up another piece of paper and glanced at it.

"Reports have reached us," said the news-reader, "concerning a gigantic monster that is terrorizing parts of the country."

"Terrorizing!" scoffed Henry. "Crikey!"

"Shush!" said Emily.

"The monster, which some eyewitnesses have described as a dinosaur, appeared in Staplewood this afternoon," continued the news-reader. "It seriously disrupted a Grand Procession that was taking place through the town centre. The monster disappeared and has not been seen since. There are no plans at the moment to re-stage the cancelled procession."

Albert tut-tutted as he leant forward and switched off the television set. "What a terrible waste of time and money!" he said. "All those months getting all

170

those floats ready—why, it took me three weekends alone to paint that Oliver Twist!"

"I know, dear," said Emily Hollins, sympathetically.

"It's face was too red," said Auntie Gertie, "even if it was supposed to be sunburnt, it was still too red."

Albert chose to ignore her remarks, and contented himself with flashing her a sour glance.

"I don't know how they can say that the *Anatosaurus* disrupted anything," said Henry.

"The Anato-what-did-you-say?" asked his father.

"I mean that monster," said Henry, quickly correcting himself. "What I mean is, it didn't really do any harm at all, did it? It just sat in the middle of the High Street. It was the Brass Band running away that caused all the trouble—and then Dad slamming his brakes on too quickly."

"Why, Henry!" gasped his mother. "However can you say such a thing! Your father acted with foresight and perspicacity! Goodness only knows *what* might have happened if he hadn't pulled up when he did!"

"But it was only *because* he pulled up quickly that the Oliver Twist statue fell off the back of the float," said Henry.

"If you ask me," put in Auntie Gertie, "it was a good job that Oliver Twist got broken—its face was too red, and I don't care what anybody says."

"I agree," said Uncle George.

Albert Hollins breathed in and out deeply several

171

times before he spoke. "I think it's about time you went to bed," he said to Henry.

"All right, Dad," Henry said.

Henry Hollins rose and, after saying his "goodnights", left the room. He walked slowly upstairs and into his bedroom; then, without taking off his clothes, he sat down on the edge of the bed—and thought. He had a good idea where the *Anatosaurus* was. The news-reader had said that there was no trace of it, and so Henry guessed that it must have made its way back to the spinney. He also guessed that when morning came, the police—if not the army—would be out in force, searching for the dinosaur. He knew that if they did find it, the very best it could hope for would be to be put in a cage for the rest of its life. Henry decided that it was his duty to help the dinosaur to escape. Henry Hollins went on sitting, quietly, on the edge of his bed for a long time, until the house was dark and still.

And then he rose, and tiptoed out of his bedroom.

Albert Hollins was eating his Sunday morning bacon-and-egg breakfast when the loud knock came on the kitchen door. When Albert opened the door, he had egg on his chin. Superintendent Farrington and two constables were standing outside.

"Good morning, sir," said the police superintendent. "Is this your back garden?" The officer waved at the garden path with his cane.

172

"I sincerely hope so," said Albert, who didn't like his mealtimes disturbed. "It comes right up to my back door, doesn't it?"

Superintendent Farrington sucked in both his cheeks. "I must ask you to be serious, Mr Hollins—it is Mr Hollins, isn't it?" Albert nodded, and Superintendent Farrington continued: "This is a very serious matter."

"Oh, yes?" said Albert, wondering what was going on.

"My men and myself", said the superintendent, "have just been making an examination of the spinney at the bottom of your garden. Were you aware, sir, that the area has recently been inhabited illegally by a dinosaur?"

Albert Hollins blinked and shook his head. "I hadn't got the faintest idea," he said.

"Do you have a son by the name of Henry Hollins?" asked the superintendent.

"That's right," said Albert.

"And could you tell me his whereabouts?"

"At this very moment?" said Albert.

"Yes."

"Of course I can," said Albert. "He's upstairs in his bed—he hasn't got up yet."

The corners of Superintendent Farrington's mouth jerked up a little, as if he knew something that Albert didn't. "You wouldn't care to check that statement for me, would you, sir?"

There was something about the way that the police officer spoke, that stopped Albert Hollins from arguing with him.

"Just a minute," said Albert. And then he turned and shot off through the kitchen and up the bedroom stairs. He was back again in a trice. "He's not there," said Albert.

"No, sir," said Superintendent Farrington. "We know he isn't. We've had a radio message from the County Headquarters about him."

"Where on earth is he then?" asked Albert, scratching his head.

Superintendent Farrington toyed with his cane before he spoke, poking a bit of loose cement between the brickwork round the Hollins' door. "Would it surprise you, Mr Hollins," the superintendent said at last, "to learn that, at this precise moment, your son, Henry, is travelling up the motorway sitting on a dinosaur's back?"

It did surprise Albert Hollins. "Oh my goodness gracious!" he said. "He'll create a traffic jam six miles long!"

Henry Hollins clung tightly to the neck of the *Anatosaurus* as it lurched along the motorway. Overhead, two police helicopters buzzed backwards and forwards, sometimes rising, sometimes falling, but never straying far from the moving dinosaur. Turning his head and looking back, Henry Hollins could

174

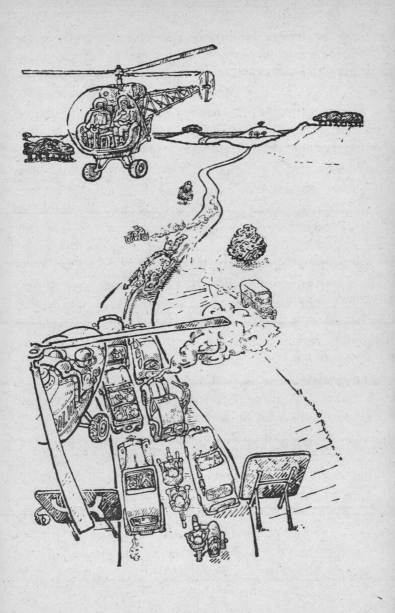

see, as Albert Hollins had so rightly predicted, a queue of impatiently honking motor vehicles that stretched away for several miles. In fact, it was this long line of traffic that was preventing the police and army authorities from catching up with and apprehending the *Anatosaurus*. At the other end of the traffic jam there were seven police cars, five army lorries, and two Chieftain tanks, all sitting it out and unable to pass.

Henry Hollins sat tight and did nothing. He was not taking the *Anatosaurus* anywhere—it was the *Anatosaurus* that was leading him on a journey of its own choosing.

The previous night, when Henry had crept out of the house and found the dinosaur in the spinney, the *Anatosaurus* had been happy to go along with Henry, wherever he chose to lead it, across the moonlit countryside. But once they had struck upon the motorway, the dinosaur had suddenly seemed to discover a mind of its own. It was then that Henry had climbed up on to the dinosaur's back, and they had been making steady progress along the motorway ever since. Henry was not *sure* where they were going, but he had a good idea that the dinosaur was heading back towards the seaside where the whole adventure had begun.

The roar of engines grew louder above his head and he could feel a stiff breeze round the back of his neck caused by a helicopter's whirling blades. Henry glanced up out of the corner of one eye and saw a policeman leaning out of one of the helicopters, a loud-hailer in his hand.

"Hey, Hollins, you down there!" the policeman bellowed. "Will you get that monster off the motorway at once, and move it over on to the hard shoulder!"

But Henry pretended that he hadn't heard and clung even tighter to the dinosaur's neck. The *Anatosaurus* padded on, steadily and surely, towards the coast.


"What worries me," said Auntie Gertie, "is what I'm going to say about this dreadful business when I next write to our Cyril."

"*Oh*, bubbles to your precious Cyril," said Emily, losing her temper with Auntie Gertie at last. "It's our poor Henry on that dinosaur's back that worries me."

Emily and Albert Hollins, Auntie Gertie and Uncle George were holding a family conference in the living-room at Woodview.

"Really, Emily!" said Auntie Gertie. "How you can speak like that I don't know! My Cyril wouldn't go causing traffic jams on the motorway and riding on dinosaurs. If your Henry had paid a little more attention to my Cyril's example, he wouldn't be in the mess he's in now!"

"Quite right," agreed Uncle George.

"I do wish you'd shut up!" said Albert, holding a

177

transistor radio to his ear and twiddling the knobs. "They're supposed to be sending out news reports about Henry from all the major road junctions on the motorway."

"Don't you tell me to shut up, Albert Hollins," said Auntie Gertie. "I've a perfect right to speak my mind. All this isn't going to do our Cyril's career any good, you know, if it gets into the Canadian newspapers."

"I said 'shut up' and I mean shut up," said Albert, flinging the transistor down in anger. "I'm fed up to the back teeth with hearing about your Cyril! I don't know why you don't go out to Canada and join him, if he's so wonderful and marvellous!"

"Well!" gasped Auntie Gertie.

"I mean it," said Albert. "Never mind about your Cyril—what about our Henry? Our Henry hatched a dinosaur egg. Something that's never been done before. And if that's not better than chopping down trees, I'll eat a plaster goose!"

"I'm not stopping here to be insulted!" said Auntie Gertie.

"Neither am I," said Uncle George.

"Buzz off then," said Albert Hollins. "You can't stay here anyway. Because I'm getting in my car and I'm off to wherever that dinosaur's going with my son."

"Now that *is* a good idea," said Emily. "I'll come with you."

"All right," said Albert. "Why don't you make up a

few sandwiches to take with us? It might be a long job. Some Spam and lettuce and a few cheese and onion would go down a treat."

"I've got a couple of custard tarts as well," said Emily. "I'll pop them in."

"Just the job!" said Albert.

Emily Hollins trotted off into the kitchen.

The ebbing tide slapped lazily along the wet sand. The afternoon sun was stealing across the sky towards the horizon. The dinosaur, with the boy now walking at its side, stumbled wearily across the last few yards of loose, soft beach and moved on to the hard, packed sand that stretched to the gently lapping sea. It had been a long and tiring journey but they were here at last.

Henry Hollins turned his eyes up to the sky. The helicopters were with them still, circling noisily in broad sweeps overhead like giant buzzing midges. He turned again and looked now at the top of the cliffs and saw two Chieftain tanks grinding to a halt, their big guns pointing down at the beach. A heavy mobile gun trundled along the cliff-top, and lined up beside the tanks. And then alongside the mobile gun came half a dozen police cars, a rocket-firing anti-tank vehicle, and a couple of Commando jeeps.

Moving his head and looking back along the row of vehicles, Henry saw that a television Outside Broadcast van had drawn up on the other side of the

Chieftain tanks. Two men were setting up a television camera and, with them, there stood a short, tubby man who was waving his arms about excitedly. Henry recognized him at once. It was Julian Derwent-Smith. And then another man joined them. A tall man whose hair seemed to stand out in spikes all over his head.

"Professor Horace Corrigan!" Henry said to himself, adding, "Now perhaps he'll believe it was a dinosaur's egg."

The cliff-top was filling up with all kinds of vehicles for as far as Henry could see. There was no escape now from the beach.

"Well, old lad," said Henry to the *Anatosaurus*, "we managed to get here, but I don't know how we're going to get away again."

But the *Anatosaurus* didn't seem to care. It was nibbling contentedly at a patch of seaweed that had been washed up on the sand, and was paying scant attention to what was happening on the cliffs.

"Henry Hollins! Henry Hollins! Can you hear me!" The words boomed down from a man in a police uniform who was shouting through a loud-hailer on the cliff-top. From the way the sun was glinting on the man's shoulder-badges, Henry guessed that he must be a very high-ranking officer indeed. Henry shaded his eyes and peered up at the cliffs but made no reply. "I want you to listen carefully and do just as I say," the man continued.

"Don't make any sudden movements, but start to walk—slowly—away from the monster and towards us. Try not to alarm the monster and it won't attack you."

"Attack me! Some hopes!" scoffed Henry to himself. Instead of walking away from the dinosaur, the boy moved closer towards it, giving it a friendly slap across the rear. "You've never attacked anything in your life except the odd lettuce, have you, Nat?"

Up on the cliff-top, the police commissioner with the loud-hailer was getting impatient. He knew that he would have to do something before it started to get dark. He had to attend an official Police Dinner that same night. Before he could go to the dinner he would have to go home and change into his best uniform. Time was all-important to him.

"Henry Hollins! Can you hear me!" the police commissioner yelled down again.

"I don't think he can, Commissioner," said an army general who was standing near by. "How about letting one of my helicopters get close in and drop a ladder for the boy to climb up?"

The police commissioner, who had already given up any hope of getting to his dinner in time for the soup course, was ready to try anything. "Go ahead," he said.

Down on the beach, Henry Hollins looked up at the sky as one of the helicopters peeled off from its two companions and swooped down with roaring engines towards the beach. The dinosaur looked up too, seaweed dangling from its jaws, and blinked at the noisy, hovering aircraft. A door opened in the helicopter's side and a nylon ladder dropped down and trailed low across the beach as the whirring machine moved in for a rescue attempt.

The ladder brushed across the leathery hide of the *Anatosaurus*, and the dinosaur grabbed at it with both front paws. Then, mistaking the nylon ladder for a length of trailing vine perhaps, the *Anatosaurus* stuffed the end of it in its mouth. Two thousand pin-point teeth nibbled on nylon while the helicopter tugged at the ladder from above.

Inside the helicopter's cabin, the pilot, Captain Nigel Threadgold, revved at his engines for full upward thrust. Down on the beach, the dinosaur, enjoying the game, tugged all the harder like a kitten hanging on a strand of wool.

On top of the cliff, the army general watched the contest through a pair of binoculars and spluttered indignantly. "The ugly brute's got me helicopter!" he said.

Down on the beach, Henry Hollins appealed to the *Anatosaurus*. "Drop it, boy! Drop it, there's a good dinosaur!" he said. But the *Anatosaurus* was having far too good a time to pay any attention to Henry, and it tugged at the nylon ladder with all of its prehistoric strength.

Up on the cliff-top, the police commissioner

182

glanced at his watch as his stomach made rumbling noises. Not only was he going to miss the soup, at this rate he looked like missing the Dover Sole course as well. The police commissioner was particularly fond of Dover Sole. "All this is getting us precisely nowhere," he grumbled.

The army general lowered his binoculars. "We'll have to show the beast that we mean business," he said, and he waved across at the artillery officer in charge of the rocket-firing anti-tank vehicle. "Give the brute a warning shot across its beam, Major!" he shouted.

The artillery major had been in charge of the rocket-firing anti-tank vehicle for over three years, but this was the first chance he had ever had to fire the weapon in earnest. In his enthusiasm, he ordered a whole salvo of rockets to be fired at once.

"sweeeoooaaaAAAAWOOO*OOOSSSHHH!*"

Five rockets blazed as one from the launchers of the anti-tank vehicle and howled across the beach no more than a dozen yards from the *Anatosaurus's* head.

The noise was ten times louder than the sound of the fighter jets that had terrified the dinosaur the day before.

The *Anatosaurus* let go of the nylon ladder and, exactly as it had done the previous day, reared up on its hind legs, stood rigid with fright for several seconds, and then threw back its bony head and let out a terrified cry. Then, as if experiencing a

183

prehistoric impulse, the dinosaur took to its thick, sturdy legs and hurtled across the beach and into the sea.

Henry watched for several seconds, frozen with horror, then, finding his legs, he ran across the sand in pursuit of the dinosaur. "Come back! Come back!" he cried. But the *Anatosaurus* was swimming with strong, natural strokes, farther and farther out to sea.

"Oh please, *please* come back!" called Henry.

But already the dinosaur was out of earshot. Its flat bony head, no larger now than the head of a pin, bobbed up and down, and up and down, and then it disappeared completely in the distant billows.

# 13

Henry Hollins watched the last military vehicle back out, away from the cliff-top, and then turn and lumber off. He could see the television camera crew packing their equipment away in the Outside Broadcast van. And then Henry realized that he was not alone on the beach. A tall man with spiky hair was running and stumbling across the sand towards him.

"Hello, Henry," gasped Professor Corrigan, arriving panting at Henry's side.

Henry said nothing. He didn't even look at the professor, but turned his eyes back out to sea. Henry was biting back tears.

The professor too fell silent. And they stood there, the boy and the man, gazing out towards the spot where the dinosaur had last been seen.

"It was an *Anatosaurus*, wasn't it?" asked the professor at last, unable to hold back the question any longer.

"Yes, it was," Henry blurted out. "And it came out of the egg that you said wasn't an egg."

"I'm sorry," said Professor Corrigan.

"It will never come back," said Henry.

"It might," said the professor.

"No." Henry shook his head. "It'll swim right out to sea and drown."

"It *might* come back," said the professor. "It was a very good swimmer the *Anatosaurus*—as at home in water as on land. It certainly won't drown. And it just might come back."

And now Henry did turn, blinking away his tears, and he looked the professor straight in the face. "Why should it?" he said. "What for? For you to shoot rockets at it?"

"That wasn't me," said Professor Corrigan. "And it was a mistake—I'm sorry."

"You keep on saying that," said Henry.

Professor Corrigan nodded and turned away, for there was nothing else that he could say. Albert and Emily Hollins had also walked across the beach and were standing a few yards away. They walked across and stood close by Henry as Professor Corrigan moved away.

"Hello, Henry," said Albert, awkwardly.

"Hello, Henry," said Emily.

"I heard what you said to that Professor Whatsisname," said Albert. "And I just want to let you know that I agree with every word you say. But he's right too, Henry, it just might come back again."

"You wouldn't let me keep it if it did," said Henry.

"How do you know", said Albert, "until you've asked?"

"Because you wouldn't let me keep it the first time," said Henry.

"I didn't even know you had it the first time," said Albert.

"You wouldn't even let me keep the egg when I had that," said Henry.

"No, that's true," said Albert, carefully. "But if it all happened again, I would the next time. I'd let you keep it in the garden. Or in the spinney, Henry. I bet I could *buy* that spinney cheap. It's not much good for anything, that spinney, except keeping dinosaurs in."

"It's easy for you to say that", said Henry, and now the tears were rolling down his cheeks, "after it's gone. And it won't come back—ever."

"Well, that's what I was thinking about," said Albert, "while you were taking to Professor Whoseit. I mean, that dinosaur out there, swimming about all on its lonesome. It might come back, if it had something to come back *for*."

"How do you mean?" said Henry.

Albert paused, and looked around the beach. "Do you recognize this place, Henry?" he said. "This is just about the spot where we had that picnic. And over there, on that ledge, is where you found that eggy thing."

"What about it?" said Henry.

"Well, what's been bothering me," said Albert, "I mean, what I'm trying to fathom out is—did dinosaurs only lay one egg at a time?"

"No," said Henry. "About seven or eight, perhaps even more than that."

"Well then," said Albert, "just supposing we were to go back up to that ledge and start to dig?"

"You and me, Dad?" said Henry.

"Why not?" said Albert. "We might come across another of those eggy things, or even two or three. More, perhaps. Then supposing we took them home? And if *they* hatched out? And, when they started to grow a bit, we brought them down here for the weekends. Well then, the one that's out there somewhere now, swimming about, on its own—what I'm trying to say, is, it *must* be lonely being millions and millions of years out of your proper time. That stands to reason, doesn't it?"

Henry nodded firmly, agreeing.

"Well then," Albert continued, "if things did work out, and there were some others of its kind about, it *would* come back then, wouldn't it, as like as not?"

"I see what your father means, Henry," said Emily.

Henry gave the matter some thought. "Even if we did," he said at last, "they'd only try to take them away from us again."

"Let 'em try!" said Albert, with a wink. "What's in my garden is my own affair—or in my spinney, come to that. What do you say, Henry? Shall we have a try and look for those eggs?"

Henry managed a wan smile; but it *was* a smile at least. "Do you mean now?" he said. "Right away?"

"Why not?" said Albert.

"Do you know what time it is?" said Henry. "What about getting home?"

"Who cares?" said his father.

"The road will be jam-packed with traffic if we don't set off soon," said Henry.

"So what?" said his father. "Why bother about traffic when you're enjoying yourself? Unless . . .?" Mr Hollins paused and looked at his wife, uncertainly. ". . . Unless there's anything you need to get back to Staplewood for, Emily?"

"Not a thing," said Mrs Hollins.

"What?" said Mr Hollins, in some surprise. "No envelopes to address? No soup-tin labels to count up on behalf of poverty-stricken panda bears? No dish-cloths that need to be knitted for pygmies in Central Africa?" Mrs Hollins shook her head, happily, and Albert Hollins could not believe his eyes. "No charitable works to catch up with *at all?*" he said.

"Charity", said Emily Hollins, with a broad smile, "begins at home. Let's go look for dinosaur eggs."

"Oh, yes, *please*, let's," said Henry, tucking one hand through his father's right arm and another hand through his mother's left arm.

Albert Hollins, his wife, Emily, and their son, Henry, all three arm-in-arm, scampered across the wet, warm sand together, across to where the white cliff rose up towards a rocky narrow ledge.

# TARGET STORY BOOKS

## Adventure

|        |                          |      |         |     |
|--------|--------------------------|------|---------|-----|
|        | Gordon Boshell           |      |         |     |
| 113918 | **THE BLACK MERCEDES**   |      |         | 60p |
| 114043 | **THE MILLION POUND RANSOM** |  |         | 60p |
| 117468 | **THE MENDIP MONEY-MAKERS** |   |         | 60p |

## Animal Stories

|        |                          |      |         |     |
|--------|--------------------------|------|---------|-----|
|        | Molly Burkett            |      |         |     |
| 118502 | **FOXES, OWLS AND ALL**  | (NF) | (illus) | 70p |
| 111567 | **THAT MAD, BAD BADGER . . .** | (NF) | (illus) | 35p |
|        | Constance Taber Colby    |      |         |     |
| 109899 | **A SKUNK IN THE FAMILY** | (NF) | (illus) | 45p |
|        | I. J. Edmonds            |      |         |     |
| 20011X | **LASSIE: THE WILD MOUNTAIN TRAIL** |  |  | 60p |
|        | G. D. Griffiths          |      |         |     |
| 113675 | **ABANDONED!**           |      | (illus) | 50p |
|        | David Gross              |      |         |     |
| 117549 | **THE BADGERS OF BADGER HILL** |  | (illus) | 50p |
|        | Michael Maguire          |      |         |     |
| 118774 | **MYLOR, THE MOST POWERFUL HORSE IN THE WORLD** |  | (illus) | 60p |
|        | Joyce Stranger           |      |         |     |
| 11017X | **THE SECRET HERDS**     |      | (illus) | 45p |
| 110099 | **THE HARE AT DARK HOLLOW** |  | (illus) | 40p |

## Mystery And Suspense

|        |                          |      |         |      |
|--------|--------------------------|------|---------|------|
|        | Ruth M. Arthur           |      |         |      |
| 111648 | **THE AUTUMN GHOSTS**    |      | (illus) | 50p  |
| 111729 | **THE CANDLEMAS MYSTERY** |    | (illus) | 45p* |
|        | Tim Dinsdale             |      |         |      |
| 105915 | **THE STORY OF THE LOCH NESS MONSTER** |  | (illus) | 50p |
|        | Leonard Gribble          |      |         |      |
| 104285 | **FAMOUS HISTORICAL MYSTERIES** | (NF) | (illus) | 50p |
|        | Alfred Hitchcock (Editor) |     |         |      |
| 117387 | **ALFRED HITCHCOCK'S TALES OF TERROR AND SUSPENSE** |  |  | 60p |
|        | Mollie Hunter            |      |         |      |
| 113756 | **THE WALKING STONES**   |      | (illus) | 45p* |
|        | Freya Littledale         |      |         |      |
| 107357 | **GHOSTS AND SPIRITS OF MANY LANDS** |  | (illus) | 50p |

†For sale in Britain and Ireland only.
*Not for sale in Canada.
♦ Film & T.V. tie-ins.

# TARGET STORY BOOKS

## Fantasy And General Fiction

| | | | | |
|---|---|---|---|---|
| | 101537 | Elisabeth Beresford<br>**AWKWARD MAGIC** | (illus) | 60p |
| | 10479X | **SEA-GREEN MAGIC** | (illus) | 60p |
| | 101618 | **TRAVELLING MAGIC** | (illus) | 60p |
| | 119142 | Eileen Dunlop<br>**ROBINSHEUGH** | (illus) | 60p |
| | 112288 | Maria Gripe<br>**THE GLASSBLOWER'S CHILDREN** | (illus) | 45p |
| | 117891 | Joyce Nicholson<br>**FREEDOM FOR PRISCILLA** | | 70p |
| | 106989 | Hilary Seton<br>**THE HUMBLES** | (illus) | 50p |
| | 109112 | **THE NOEL STREATFEILD CHRISTMAS HOLIDAY BOOK** | (illus) | 60p |
| | 109031 | **THE NOEL STREATFEILD EASTER HOLIDAY BOOK** | (illus) | 60p |
| | 105249 | **THE NOEL STREATFEILD SUMMER HOLIDAY BOOK** | (illus) | 50p |

## Humour

| | | | | |
|---|---|---|---|---|
| | 107519 | Eleanor Estes<br>**THE WITCH FAMILY** | (illus) | 50p |
| | 11762X | Felice Holman<br>**THE WITCH ON THE CORNER** | (illus) | 50p |
| | 105672 | Spike Milligan<br>**BADJELLY THE WITCH** | (illus) | 60p |
| | 109546 | **DIP THE PUPPY** | (illus) | 60p |
| | 107438 | Christine Nostlinger<br>**THE CUCUMBER KING** | (illus) | 45p |
| | 119223 | Mary Rogers<br>**A BILLION FOR BORIS** | | 60p |

## 0426    Film And TV Tie-ins

| | | | | |
|---|---|---|---|---|
| 200187 | Kathleen N. Daly<br>**RAGGEDY ANN AND ANDY** (Colour illus) | 75p ♦ * |
| 11826X | John Ryder Hall<br>**SINBAD AND THE EYE OF THE TIGER** | 70p* ♦ |
| 11535X | John Lacarotti<br>**OPERATION PATCH** | 45p |
| 119495 | Pat Sandys<br>**THE PAPER LADS** | 60p ♦ |
| 115511 | Alison Thomas<br>**BENJI** | 40p |

† For sale in Britain and Ireland only.
* Not for sale in Canada.
♦ Film & T.V. tie-ins.

Wyndham Books are obtainable from many booksellers and newsagents. If you have any difficulty please send purchase price plus postage on the scale below to:

**Wyndham Cash Sales**
**P.O. Box 11**
**Falmouth**
**Cornwall**

While every effort is made to keep prices low, it is sometimes necessary to increase prices at short notice. Wyndham Books reserve the right to show new retail prices on covers which may differ from those advertised in the text or elsewhere.

## Postage and Packing Rate

**UK:** 22p for the first book, plus 10p per copy for each additional book ordered to a maximum charge of 82p. **BFPO and Eire:** 22p for the first book, plus 10p per copy for the next 6 books and thereafter 4p per book. **Overseas:** 30p for the first book and 10p per copy for each additional book.

These charges are subject to Post Office charge fluctuations.